I0600445

Quiet Summer

A Comedy in Three Acts

by Marrijane Hayes
and
Joseph Hayes

A SAMUEL FRENCH ACTING EDITION

SAMUEL FRENCH

FOUNDED 1830

New York Hollywood London Toronto

SAMUELFRENCH.COM

QUIET SUMMER

STORY OF THE PLAY

A new play by the authors of *And Came the Spring, Life of the Party, Come Rain or Shine, Come Over to Our House,* and other hilarious hits for the school theatre. Like all of the authors' previous plays, *Quiet Summer* is a fast-moving, rollicking comedy with an interesting and amusing theme. In this play it is summer. And James Clark, lawyer, has hopes of spending it in peace and serenity, concentrating on getting elected president of his country-club—knowing that this will be the first step toward winning his race for District Attorney in the fall. But the best laid plans of men who are uncles often go astray. And James is an uncle. His sister Lillian and her husband want a summer away from Pamela, 17, and Sonny, 15, so the kids arrive from New York to stay with Uncle Jimmie. In the course of three uproarious acts Uncle Jimmie learns about the younger generation and he learns to relax; he even wins his election—through the inventive and unconventional aid of the kids and the helpers they quickly gather around them. But before these pleasant developments, Pamela and Sonny, working at breakneck speed, get involved in romantic (almost marital) adventures, they all but smash James' happy romance, they turn his home into a combination rumpus-room and campaign-headquarters; and they manage to learn a few things themselves along their merry way. All this —and much more—is presented in the same cheerful, swift and humorous manner, complete with surprises, that made the earlier plays by these authors such outstanding successes all over the country.

CAST OF CHARACTERS
(8 Males, 10 Females)

PAMELA YOUNG
HELEN RUSSELL
JEANIE DAY
HARRIET MORGAN
BETSY HARRISON
ESTHER HAMILTON
MRS. LILLIAN YOUNG
FREDERICKA COLLINS
FRANCES SHAUGHNESSY
CARRIE

MR. JAMES CLARK
SONNY YOUNG
BILL HENLY
MR. LESLIE GARDNER
MR. CLIFFORD YOUNG
TUBBY PITTS
TONY
MR. HENRY MORGAN

ACTION AND SCENE

*The scene throughout is the study in the home of James
Clark in the country near a medium-sized midwestern town.*

ACT ONE: *A Tuesday afternoon in early July.*

ACT TWO:
SCENE 1: *The following Saturday evening, around
seven-thirty.*

SCENE 2: *One week later—Saturday, just after
noon.*

ACT THREE: *Several hours later.*

5

QUIET SUMMER

ACT ONE

SCENE: *The study in James Clark's house in the country near a medium-sized midwestern town.*

JAMES CLARK is a bachelor; he is also an attorney. As such, he has a study. He is also an uncle—and as such he has a niece and a nephew. What concerns us at the moment is his study.

It is a large, comfortable, masculine room, used as a living room most of the time; at first glance, rather somber, but this is somewhat relieved by bright pillows and drapes.

In the down Left wall is a door leading to the more formal living room and the other parts of the house. The up Left corner of the room is a step above floor level and the front hall is almost a part of the study; there are no doors—just a large opening—between the two. In the rear wall of the hall —within sight of the audience—is the front door (a strong, practical "slam" door). In the hall also is the stairway; the audience can see one newel post, the railing and three or four lower steps.

The rear wall of the room is formed by a huge fireplace flanked by two high, draped windows. Above the fireplace are prints and trophies and crossed fencing foils—possibly a framed fish.

The up Right corner, also a step above floor level to correspond with the up Left corner, is cut off, and French doors are set at an angle joining the rear and Right walls.

7

The walls of the room are lined with books; most of them look pretty dull, being law tomes. There is a sofa at Right Center, facing down; and against the Right wall, downstage, is a radio-phonograph combination, a hassock in front of it. To the Left, also facing down, is a desk, with a chair behind it. Telephone on desk. Two other chairs, upstage and facing each other in front of fireplace (hereafter referred to as the up Right and up Left chairs), complete the necessary furnishings.

TIME: *A bright Tuesday afternoon in early July, with sun streaming pleasantly through the windows and the French doors.*

AT RISE: *The room presents an extremely neat appearance—a key to the personality of its owner.*

That owner, JAMES CLARK, *is pacing up and down at the moment, a desk-calendar in his hand. JAMES is not quite thirty-five, but already he has begun a fight against encroaching plumpness, especially around the mid-section. He is a man accustomed to—and desiring—a well-regulated, well-organized life. A lawyer by profession, he sometimes has trouble remembering, especially in moments of stress, that he is not addressing a jury. In his own inflated opinion of himself, he is warm, open-hearted, kindly, worldly, understanding; this conception forms an attitude that might be more irritating in a person of less genuine personal charm. And he can't really help it that he's just a trifle pompous.*

HELEN RUSSELL *is behind desk, at typewriter; she is an attractive bachelor-girl who has just turned thirty. She has a brisk, fertile mind. She is quite a pleasant person with a protective sense of humor and a mind a trifle more realistic than* JAMES'. *She is his secretary and she is his girl-friend. The two occupations sometimes become tangled. At the moment she holds a telegram in her hand.*

JAMES. Read it to me again.

HELEN. *(Reading)* "Pamela and Sonny have been talking about their Uncle Jim so much lately that we have decided to let them visit you while we continue our trip to Mexico." Signed—"Your loving sister, Lillian." *(She looks up)* I know it by heart.

JAMES. Just like Lillian—she doesn't say *when!* I hate women with fluttery minds. *(Crosses to* HELEN*)* Thank heaven you don't have a fluttery mind, Helen.

HELEN. Mister Clark—remember: I'm your secretary.

JAMES. *(Stepping back)* Oh— Well, of course I *know* you're my secretary.

HELEN. And when I took this job—not eight years ago—you said we could never mix business with pleasure.

JAMES. Don't keep reminding me what I said eight years ago. I was very young.

HELEN. We're not getting any younger, James. Eight years—and then seven years ago, look what happened. You took me to the movies.

JAMES. *(Smiling at her)* I remember. "The Case of the Stuttering Bishop." A very implausible picture.

HELEN. Seven years ago. You waited a whole year —and I've been waiting ever since.

JAMES. *(Very business-like suddenly, claps his hands together and walks to Right)* Hmmm— Take a letter— No, take a telegram— Maybe I better call long distance.

HELEN. All the way to New York?

JAMES. Not that I don't love my niece and nephew. Nice kids, as I remember them. Pamela has braces on her teeth and she lisps—

HELEN. Lovely—

JAMES. And—what's that boy's name?

HELEN. *(Looking at telegram again)* Sonny.

JAMES. Yeah—Sonny. I don't remember much about

him. But if he's my sister Lillian's boy, he's—he's a good kid. I mean he probably *behaves* well anyway. *(On second thought)* If he can keep his mind straight for half a minute. —Helen, I don't want any kids around here. They're always falling down and hurting themselves—and I'll be responsible. *(Suddenly angry)* What the devil does that sister of mine mean? She has no right—

(CARRIE *enters from down Left living room. She is* JAMES' *housekeeper—a large, sardonic woman, accustomed to* JAMES' *ways.*)

CARRIE. Pardon me, Mr. Clark— How old are your niece and nephew?

JAMES. Oh, Carrie—I don't know. *(His hands describe very small children in the air; he gives one of them a paternal tap on its non-existent head)* You know —children.

CARRIE. *(Shaking her head)* I mean in years— Do I have to sterilize bottles?

JAMES. Carrie, please don't be facetious. In addition to which, they're not coming—

CARRIE. Good! *(She goes out quickly, down Left.)*

JAMES. *(Thoughtfully—as he argues with himself)* I know it would be good for them. There they are— cooped up in an apartment in New York all year. And all this fresh air and sunshine going to waste— *(Then his voice changing, as he takes the other side of the argument)* But there's fresh air and sunshine in Mexico, too, isn't there? Let them go to Mexico with Lillian— *(Shifting back again)* Still—I sometimes wish there were some kids running around this house. And Mexico isn't the same as a house—with the Country Club just down the road—swimming, cowboy-and-Indian— *(He pauses.)*

HELEN. *(Drily)* Who won this time?

JAMES. *(Briskly)* I did! Take a telegram. *(He paces to up Right.* HELEN *gets notebook and pencil and takes dictation as she rises and crosses to sofa)* "Dear Lillian:

Although I am pleased to have your wire and to know that little Pamela and—" What's that boy's name?

HELEN. Sonny. *(Sits on sofa.)*

JAMES. "—To know that little Pamela and Sonny think about their poor old uncle—" Take out that "old." Just "uncle." *(He paces to Left, dictating)* "Regardless, I must inform you that my summer promises to be quite full as it is. I need not mention to you that in the fall your little brother—" Take out that "little." —"your brother has hopes of becoming the District Attorney of Somerset County. With this in mind—"

HELEN. *(Without looking up)* James—you're not addressing a jury. A telegram costs by the word.

JAMES. *(Crossing to Right)* Make it a day letter. No, send it air-mail.

CARRIE. *(Re-enters from down Left)* Where will they sleep?

JAMES. Carrie, don't bother me. We have a guest room, don't we? Pamela can sleep there. And that boy— *(With a look at HELEN as she says the word at the same time)* Sonny—can sleep—well, let's see—

CARRIE. In your room, maybe. In the other twin bed.

JAMES. Carrie—I prefer to approach this whole thing in a different manner.

CARRIE. We'll put a cot up in the upstairs hall.

JAMES. We'll do nothing of the sort!

CARRIE. How long are they going to stay?

JAMES. How long does it take to go to Mexico and back?

CARRIE. Depends on how long you want to stay in Mexico.

JAMES. Carrie, sometimes I think I can't bear your logic— Sonny's a kind of nice little boy—he won't mind a little inconvenience.

CARRIE. Well, *I* will! *(She goes out again.)*

JAMES. *(Turning to HELEN)* To tell the truth—I don't even remember what Sonny looks like!

HELEN. James—I sometimes think if you're elected District Attorney, this County is going to be overrun with gangsters.

JAMES. *(Outraged)* Helen—that's a terrible thing to say! Why, I'm the best lawyer this side of the Mississippi! And you know it!

HELEN. *(Smiling)* Are they coming or aren't they?

JAMES. I've just been thinking—you know, it might be pleasant to have a flock of kids all over the house. Sometimes it almost makes me wish I'd married, myself, and—

HELEN. That's not a proposal, is it, James?

JAMES. *(Flustered, retreating from her)* Now, Helen, now—let's not make this personal, you know. I mean—let's keep this abstract. Time—

HELEN. —Heals all wounds. I know.

JAMES. *(Walking away from her to Right)* You finish the letter, Helen. You know what to say— The answer is *no*. Make Lillian understand—

HELEN. *(Crossing to desk; placing paper in typewriter)* I'll finish the letter, but I'm not sure she'll understand.

(Looks up as JAMES *goes to select books from cases Right, until he has an armful.)*

JAMES. Now these are the books I have to read this summer. *(Places them on top of radio)* With court not in session, it's a good chance. And then there's that Country-Club Presidency to think about—

HELEN. James— *(She stands up.)*

JAMES. *(Turning—surprised)* What?

HELEN. James—I think you should let those children come.

JAMES. *(Surprised)* You what?

HELEN. Yes, I do. You're becoming a regular fussbudget—with every little minute laid out, your whole life so regulated and planned that you're going to end up a frustrated old man—

JAMES. *(Amazed and chagrined, going toward her)* Helen—is that the way to—?

HELEN. *(Upset)* No, it's *not* the way to talk to my

employer. But you're more than my employer. You told me you loved me—

JAMES. I do—I mean—

HELEN. I'd rather see a bomb dropped into your careful little life than anything I know! So I *won't* write your letter! And I *won't* stand around any more and watch you becoming a fidgety old man! *(Goes toward hall as* CARRIE *enters carrying a bowl of string-beans, from down Left, and stands listening)* And I want to warn you, Mister James Clark, Attorney-at-Law, that I don't intend to waste my whole life waiting until you're so old you can't wobble up the church-aisle! *(She goes up Left into hall.)*

*(*JAMES *stands staring at her, amazed. Then she goes outside and the front door SLAMS.* JAMES *leaps.* CARRIE *has a blank look.)*

CARRIE. *(Softly)* Bravo!

JAMES. *(Turning to* CARRIE*)* What did you say?

CARRIE. *(Unconcernedly)* I said—bravo. Good for her! You've had that coming for a long time.

(The DOORBELL buzzes. CARRIE *sets bowl on desk and goes into hall. She opens front door and* TONY, *the expressman, stands there, a rather large box beside him.* TONY *is a little man in his late thirties with an acid tongue and a perpetually surprised expression. He hands the delivery-pad to* CARRIE. JAMES *slumps to sofa, staring ahead, morose, be-wildered.)*

TONY. That young woman almost knocked me down. The package is insured, but I aint.

CARRIE. Bring it inside. *(Signs delivery slip.)*

TONY. *(Lifts box and brings it in and places it on floor at Center)* What's a matter—little fight in here?

CARRIE. *(In hall)* Never mind.

TONY. Okay, Miss! Don't bite my head off. I wasn't in it. (CARRIE *steps into room)* People always fightin'.

Saw a beaut this mornin'. Woman hit her husband with an umbrella. He wanted me to be a witness. I said, "Listen, Mister—I just deliver things. I aint a umpire." *(Looks back at* JAMES*)* Cheer up, Mister—anyway, she didn't use a umbrella. *(Goes into hall and out door.)*

JAMES. What is all this? I don't like it. Helen knows I don't like personal disturbances of this nature. *(Paces)* It doesn't help my digestion, either. And right now, when I should be concentrating on the Country Club election— *(Stops; looks at* CARRIE, *who is examining box)* —Did you hear what she said to me? Is that what people think of me?

CARRIE. Not people. Just us. Helen and me— We *know* you.

JAMES. What is that thing doing cluttering up my study?

CARRIE. I don't know, Mr. Clark. It's addressed to you. *(Reads label)* From the Ajax Athletic Corporation.

JAMES. *(Embarrassed, his manner changes)* Oh— Oh, well, Carrie—you go on and do whatever it is you do in the mornings—

CARRIE. *(Her interest peaked now, folds her arms, waiting)* I wasn't doing anything.

JAMES. *(Accusingly)* Yes, you were. You were shelling beans or stringing peas or something. Go on—

CARRIE. When was the last time you saw these relatives of yours, Mr. Clark?

JAMES. Can't you keep your mind on one subject at a time? I don't remember— Let's see—

CARRIE. When Hoover was President?

JAMES. How do I know who was President?

CARRIE. What I'm getting at is—these kids might be ready for marriage. Had that ever occurred to you?

JAMES. *(Struck)* Little Pamela. And—and Sonny. No, no, I tell you they're just— *(Again his hands fly through the air)* just—you know, children.

CARRIE. Well, if they are, what are we going to do about food around here?

JAMES. Carrie—you're bothering me. You're worse than Helen. Food? What do we usually do with food? We eat it.

CARRIE. I do. You don't— *(Picks up bowl)* Ever since you discovered your waistline wasn't a girlish twenty-nine, you've been starving yourself on jello and salads. Those kids—

JAMES. *(Who has stood enough—pointing dramatically)* Carrie—go to the kitchen!—And those kids—those kids aren't coming. I've sent a wire or day letter —or something—

CARRIE. *(As she starts for down Left door)* You'd think it was the Dark Ages. I am *not* a slave. *(Turns at door)* You, Mr. James Clark—remember what Helen said! *(Goes out quickly.)*

(JAMES *stands glaring after her a moment, then he goes to box and rips it open. What he discovers is an electric reducing machine. He is momentarily delighted and he tries to figure out how it works. While he is so engrossed, a CAR is heard approaching outside. Then a DOOR slams. And almost immediately a tremendous commotion is set up: dog BARKS, loud VOICES, SQUEALS of delight, GROANS, voices, more door-slamming, a HORN blowing. JAMES dashes to the windows Left Center rear and looks out. Then slowly his hand goes to his head. He turns and dashes to the down Left door, calling.)*

JAMES. Carrie! Carrie!

CARRIE. *(Appearing, drying her hands on apron)* Don't tell me all that racket comes from that little box— *(Points to reducing machine.)*

JAMES. *(In a hushed, awed, frightened voice)* Carrie—something horrible's gone wrong.

(The NOISE continues behind this.)

CARRIE. *(As she goes to window to look out)* All we

need for a circus is some music— *(As if in answer to her command, the sound of a SAXOPHONE is heard outside, very loud, playing a march.* CARRIE *shrugs)* Okay—we got a circus.

(NOTE: *If the actor playing* SONNY *is unable to play the saxophone, he can learn to play some simple tune or the scales and repeat these whenever saxophone-playing is required in the action. In some ways, this would be even more amusing because, as* PAMELA *explains, "He's just learning to play." It is not necessary for the actor to play the saxophone.)*

(The front door BUZZER sounds. CARRIE *goes to hall.)*

JAMES. *(As he crosses to Right)* No. No! They wouldn't do this to me—

(MRS. LILLIAN YOUNG *enters from hall. She is* JAMES' *sister — a flighty, slightly over-dressed, gushy woman with a sweet, sweet manner. She rushes over to* JAMES *at Right.)*

LILLIAN. Jimmie! Jimmie darling! Oh, my, I feel just like weeping. It's been so long since I saw my dear little brother— Jimmie—you look sick.
JAMES. Who's making that noise?
LILLIAN. Noise? I don't hear a thing. (JAMES *stares at her, pop-eyed, because the racket has, if anything, grown in volume)* Oh, Jimmie, you'll get used to that. He's learning to play the saxophone this summer.
JAMES. Lillian—you didn't say when you were arriving—

(During this MR. CLIFFORD YOUNG, LILLIAN'S *husband, has appeared in hall. He is leaning in entrance-way now, surveying the room. A man in his early forties, he has a constantly weary, benign,*

*overcome expression, and a soft voice; long ago he
has learned the uselessness of revolt.)*

LILLIAN. *(To* JAMES*)* We wanted to *surprise* you.
CLIFFORD. And *I* was afraid you'd change your mind.
JAMES. Change my—? I hadn't even made up my—

(Before he can finish, SONNY YOUNG *appears in hall,
playing his saxophone.* CLIFFORD *moves to up Center.* SONNY *is nearly seventeen—dressed accordingly, but always a little more so than is necessary:
brightly, flashily. His frank and friendly face gives
little clue to his inventive nature. He moves fast
and with enough enthusiasm to weary anyone past
the age of twenty-one. He finishes the tune with a
high flourish and then stands beaming, waiting for
compliments.)*

JAMES. *(In a little voice)* Who's that?
LILLIAN. Why, Jimmie—I'm ashamed of you. Not
knowing your own little nephew—
JAMES. *(Pointing)* That's not— Don't tell me that's—
SONNY. *(Going to* JAMES*)* Sonny, Uncle Jim. You've
got a nice layout here. With a few little changes, we
can pep it up and make quite a place for you. *(He is
pumping* JAMES' *limp hand)* You haven't got much of
a grip, Uncle Jim. What's the matter—law practice get
you down? *(Taps* JAMES' *midsection)* You ought to do
something about that paunch, Unc. (JAMES *quickly
pulls coat over stomach and buttons it, looking injured)*
Tells in your whole outlook. What musical instrument
do you play?

(Before JAMES *can answer these machine-gun ques-
tions,* PAMELA *appears in hall and stands on step,
surveying the room. She is trying on moods to see
how they fit. At the moment* PAMELA, *who is really
an attractive, high-spirited young lady of seventeen
and a half, has decided her heart is broken and she*

acts accordingly—in a languorous, limp way, eye-lids half closed, head back, hand on hip.)

JAMES. *(Bluntly)* What's the matter with *her?*

(PAMELA stares at him, hard.)

SONNY. *(Crossing to radio at Right)* She's in love, Unc. *(Puts saxophone on top of books on radio.)*

JAMES. Who *is* she?

LILLIAN. Pam, darling, come down here and meet your Uncle Jimmie. *(To JAMES)* Everyone loves Pam.

JAMES. *(Displeased)* I can tell.

LILLIAN. *(As she goes toward her daughter)* Pam—come here, dear, and look at your Uncle Jimmie.

PAMELA. *(Languorously, distastefully)* I can see enough from here.

CLIFFORD. *(Stepping forward)* Jim, I think we owe you an apology—

LILLIAN. *(Turning to glare at CLIFFORD)* Clifford! *(He shrugs and sits in up Left chair).* I don't know what on earth you could mean—

CARRIE. *(Crossing to behind desk and watching)* I do.

LILLIAN. *(Quickly to JAMES)* They've been so eager to see their Uncle Jimmie again. Sonny kept saying, "He was such a regular fellow."

SONNY. *(Disgusted)* Mother—the last time I saw Uncle Jim, I was exactly three years old. He kept pinching me—

LILLIAN. Sonny!

SONNY. They just figured they needed a vacation from us, Uncle Jim—and I kind of believe they're right.

LILLIAN. *(To change subject)* James—you haven't changed a bit. I'd hoped you'd be more gracious now that you're such an important lawyer. You haven't even asked us to sit down.

JAMES. *(Barking)* Sit down!

LILLIAN. *(Surprised, sits on sofa)* I could almost

cry—after all this thinking about you and worrying about you—

JAMES. *(Contrite, sits beside her—he is always baffled by women and especially women's tears)* Now, Lil, listen—I didn't mean anything, in particular. I simply thought you'd be more comfortable sitting down—

SONNY. You see, Unc—Mother and Dad think if they get away from us for a while, they'll be able to appreciate us more. It's very sound psychology. I agree.

PAMELA. Has any mail arrived for me yet?

LILLIAN. Sonny—you make everything sound so—horrible.

CLIFFORD. He's right.

LILLIAN. *(Turning)* Clifford!

CLIFFORD. *(Subsiding again)* Sorry.

PAMELA. No one has answered my question.

SONNY. *(To JAMES)* Pam's mooning about some boys in New York. She thinks all her nice girl friends will take her nice boy friends away from her this summer —and she's probably right.

JAMES. *(To SONNY)* Is anyone ever *wrong?*

SONNY. What?

JAMES. *(Rising to face SONNY)* I want to know if anyone is ever wrong? Every time you report on what somebody thinks or says, you add, "They're right—" or "I agree." *Is anyone ever wrong?*

SONNY. Yes.

JAMES. Who?

SONNY. *You* are, if you think you can start bullying me around!

(A pause. JAMES, defeated, turns away with a baffled shrug.)

LILLIAN. *(Taking command)* Sonny, Pan—hadn't you better start unpacking the car?

SONNY. Want to help, Unc? (JAMES *glares at him.* SONNY, *seeing the fire in* JAMES' *eyes, starts to hall. As he reaches* PAMELA, *he pauses, brings his hands to his chest in a mock tragic manner and sings:)* "I wonder who's kissing him now. I wonder who's buying the cokes—"

(PAMELA *loses her attitude, her fists clench; she makes a dive for her brother, who dashes out front door.*)

PAMELA. You shut up or I'll wring your neck! *(This is such a dramatic change in* PAMELA'S *attitude that* JAMES *stares, goggle-eyed.* PAMELA *bolts after* SONNY. *The front door slams—hard!)* Some day I won't be responsible— *(She goes out front door; it slams again!)*

LILLIAN. *(To* JAMES*)* You'll love them, Jimmie—

JAMES. *(Weakly)* I'm sure of it. *(Then making up his mind)* Now you look here, Lillian—

(But before he can continue, SONNY *reappears at door, loaded down with luggage, golf clubs, and as much paraphernalia as he can manage in one trip.)*

SONNY. Where do I park these, Unc?

JAMES. *(Absently)* First door on the left upstairs— *(Then he catches himself)* No! No! You can take those things right back— *(But* SONNY *has already disappeared upstairs.* JAMES *cries out in a burst of rebellion)* But that's *my* room!

(Now PAMELA *appears in the door, similarly loaded down—tennis racquets, luggage, hat-boxes, etc.)*

LILLIAN. Take it up the stairs, Pam darling.

PAMELA. There's a lot more. *(She goes up the stairs)* The dog can sleep with me.

JAMES. Dog? Does she have a— *(The dog BARKS— outside front door.* JAMES *turns weakly to* CARRIE*)* Carrie—you'd better see that they stow those things in the right rooms. I want to be able to get to my bed tonight.

CARRIE. *(Going to hall)* Remember what I said about the food, Mr. Clark. After all this exercise—

SONNY. *(Comes down stairs and meets her at hall door; overhears this last sentence)* Did someone say food? I could eat a team of horses, wagon and all.

CARRIE. See? *(She disappears upstairs.)*

SONNY. *(Starts outside)* There's more. I think we better use the French doors—more room. *(He goes.)*

JAMES. *(To LILLIAN)* Listen to me, Lillian. Right this minute I'm waiting for word. There's a meeting this afternoon to nominate the two men who are going to run for the presidency of my Country Club.

LILLIAN. Isn't that nice, Jimmie? I hope you win.

JAMES. You don't understand. If I'm nominated, that means I have to do some very clever campaigning. That Country Club election means more to me—

SONNY. *(Loaded as before, stands at French doors Right)* Did you say Country Club, Unc? Do you play golf? I'll beat the socks off you! *(Crosses to hall and disappears up the stairs.)*

JAMES. *(His hand through his hair, through tight teeth)* Lillian—what I'm trying to say is that it's *more* than a Country Club election. You see, if I'm elected, it will mean every member of the Club will support me for the District Attorney's office in the fall. *(Beginning to make a speech again—at Center)* I don't mean to boast, but I might say, with due modesty—

PAMELA. *(Now reappears coming down stairs. She stands in the hall archway)* How far are we from town out in this no-man's land, Uncle Jimmie?

JAMES. Two miles. And this is hardly no-man's land!

PAMELA. Where's the swimming pool?

JAMES. At the Club. Less than a mile away.

PAMELA. A mile?! And no subways! *(Turns to go.)*

SONNY. *(Reappears and goes out for still another load, singing as he passes his sister)* "I wonder who's kissing him now—I wonder who's showing him how—"

(PAMELA throws her head in the air and follows SONNY out front door.)

JAMES. That election means a great deal to me, Lillian. And I'm of the opinion—I might even say the sincere and heartfelt opinion—that these kids aren't going to be any genuine help—

LILLIAN. Oh, Jimmie—you don't know them. They'll help in every way imaginable. *(Turns to* CLIFFORD*)* Clifford—are you ready? We have a long drive in front of us, Jimmie—

CLIFFORD. Oh, we'll make good time now. The car's a lot lighter.

*(*SONNY *appears in French doors again with still another large load. This time a portable radio is in full view, very large and conspicuous. He starts for hall, as* CARRIE *comes down stairs.)*

SONNY. Pam's bringing the records. *(Sets radio down by fireplace)* —Say, Unc, what I want to know is: are there any interesting people around here? Pam's mooning around but I'm fancy-free and ready for love.

*(*CARRIE *stands in hall.)*

JAMES. What?

SONNY. *(Explaining, trying to be patient)* Love. You know—hubba-hubba. The smoocheroola. Slick chicks passing the honey to me, baby— Holy Jeepers—don't tell me you never heard of love out here!

CARRIE. Mr. Clark thought you'd be interested in cowboys and Indians.

SONNY. I'm not interested in cowboys but an Indian might take my fancy—if she's pretty enough. *(Continues to hall.)*

CLIFFORD. *(Stops him. Rises)* Hey—that's mine! *(Goes to* SONNY *and disentangles a suitcase.)*

SONNY. Sorry, Pop. They ˜˜ouldn't fit me anyway. *(Goes off and up stairs.)*

*(*CLIFFORD, *with suitcase, stands waiting, as* LILLIAN *prepares to take her leave.)*

JAMES. Lillian! Lillian—you can't go. You can't leave me—at the mercy of these—these—these— *(He can't find the word.)*

CLIFFORD. *(Going to* JAMES *and taking his hand)* I know just what you mean.

LILLIAN. Clifford! What a thing to say about your own children!

*(*PAMELA *appears again at French doors with another load.)*

JAMES. *(Hand to head) Where's all that stuff coming from?*

CARRIE. That's not the question. You should see where it's going. (JAMES *stares at her)* The upstairs is beginning to look like a high school gymnasium.

*(*PAMELA *crosses to up Left during following)*

CLIFFORD. It's all coming from the car, Jim. You see, I drove and Lillian sat next to me. Pamela sat on the other side of her, with the radio and typewriter in between—Sonny curled up on top of everything in the back seat with his head near the ceiling. He complained every time we hit a bump.

PAMELA. Uncle Jimmie—we can't sit around this *library* all summer, you know. What do you have planned for us?

LILLIAN. Now, Pam—your uncle will be very busy and he'll need peace and quiet so he can work. I expect you and Sonny to behave exactly as if your mother and father were here.

CLIFFORD. Not *exactly,* Pam— Have a heart.

LILLIAN. Clifford! I'll speak to you later!

CLIFFORD. I'll keep quiet, Lillian.—If only you won't "speak to me" all the way to Mexico and back. *(Turns to* JAMES*)* When your sister gets started, Jim—I sideswipe other cars.

PAMELA. *(Going into hall and upstairs)* I've got a feeling this is going to be a morgue all summer.

JAMES. I've got a feeling she's right.

LILLIAN. *(Going to hall and singing out)* Children, children—come down now and kiss us goodbye. We're leaving.

JAMES. *(Crosses to face* LILLIAN*)* What did I ever do to you? What did I ever do to deserve—

(The TELEPHONE rings on desk. CARRIE *answers.)*

CARRIE. Hello! James Clark's residence— I beg your pardon?

LILLIAN. *(To* JAMES*)* You'll thank me for this some day. Why, just looking at this room, I can tell you're becoming an old bachelor—

CARRIE. *(Loud)* I can't hear a word.

LILLIAN. I said he was becoming a staid, stiff old bachelor.

CARRIE. I agree with you. But I can't hear what this man's saying to me on the telephone.

LILLIAN. Oh, I thought you said—

CLIFFORD. Lillian—never mind.

CARRIE. *(Into telephone)* Hello? What? A call to *where? (Looks up)* Did you place a call to New York, Mr. Clark?

JAMES. New York? No, I—

PAMELA. *(Tearing down stairs and into room)* That's mine, that's mine! *(Catches herself and becomes again the languorous lady with the drooping lids)* Oh, I do believe that's my call—if you don't mind.

CARRIE. *(Handing her the telephone)* Well, it's not mine. Some man keeps saying, "Is that you, my darling lonesome droolsome?"

PAMELA. *(Archly—into phone)* Hello?—Oh, yes, Jeffrey. Yes, this is—*she*— Well, you see, there was some confusion. I placed the call from the upstairs phone and the maid didn't know it—

CARRIE. *(As she comes down Left)* Maid? I'm a housekeeper!

(SONNY enters in hall from upstairs and stands near PAMELA.)

PAMELA. *(Ignoring this)* I was just—you know—wondering— You see, there's a big party here—and some nice boy keeps plucking at my arm— *(In another voice—to impress* JEFFREY. SONNY *plucks her arm after he looks around, mockingly, and sees that he is the only "nice boy" around her)* Jimmie, will you stop?

JAMES. Me? *Me?* What did *I* do?

SONNY. Shh—listen and learn something, Unc. *(He gets his face pretty close to the telephone, an expression of sublime mockery on it.)*

PAMELA. Yes—a *big* party. A kind of welcome, I guess— *(Glances at* JAMES*)* Oh, him—well, for one thing, he's awfully *young*—for an uncle. And kind of handsome. And he knows all sorts of really *adult* men to introduce me to. Really *handsome* adult men, *sophisticated*—

JAMES. Hah!

CARRIE. *(To* JAMES*)* You may as well enjoy this, Mr. Clark—you're paying for it.

JAMES. Paying?! Say—

PAMELA. *(Into telephone)* I tell you it's a party. I can hardly understand a *word* you're saying, Jeffrey.

SONNY. *(Bursting into song—to give the party-effect)* "How are things in Glocca-Morra?" *(Dashes to Right and gets his saxophone from radio and starts playing very softly—background music—as he returns to desk.)*

PAMELA. Oh, it's grand—listen, will you? (SONNY, *obliging, toots very loud.* PAMELA *gives a false little laugh)* There!—Well, I just wanted you to know I'm having a good time—with men and boys all over the place. And so *attentive. (Her voice changing)* And what are you doing, Jeffrey? *(Listens)* With who—? *(Suddenly getting very angry)* With *her?* Jeffrey Campbell—do you mean to stand there and tell me you're taking some *other* girl to the theatre? (SONNY *plays a sad, sour note on saxophone)* Well, all I can say is—you're about the most fickle, untrue, deceitful and *contemptible* person I've ever heard of and I just hope I never see you again as long as I live on this foul and *contemptible* earth! Goodbye! *(But she doesn't hang up; she waits. Then her eyes widen. Then she replaces telephone and her voice rises in a terrible screech) He* hung up! He hung up on me! *(Picks up telephone, really angry, with tears)* Operator, Operator —get me that number in New York again!

JAMES. *(Also something of a wail)* No! *(Crosses to telephone and places hand on hook)* No! Now you listen to me, young lady—

PAMELA. *(Turning on* JAMES*)* Oh, you—you grouchy old man! You mean, stingy, *contemptible— (Starts for* LILLIAN, *kisses her once)* Now I hope you see what you're doing to your daughter—ruining her whole life! *(Crosses to* CLIFFORD *to kiss him)* And you stand around and let her! *(Facing them all—tragically)* My whole life is going to pot! *(Spelling it to make sure they get it)* P-o-t—pot! Buried here in this wilderness in the *absolutely most important summer* of my whole life. You're all against me. I'll end up an *old maid* sitting around knitting sweaters for Sonny's little girl! *(With this, she bolts out of the room and into hall and upstairs.)*

SONNY. *(Following her to hall arch) What* little girl? Pam—you're years and years ahead of yourself. *(Turns to room—throwing up hands and shrugging)* Now see what you've done? I've got a family already.

(Outside the front door a DOG begins to howl—long, mournful, loud. JAMES, *who has crossed to hall to stare abstractedly up the stairs after* PAMELA, *turns to face room.)*

JAMES. Do you hear that?

LILLIAN. *(Innocently)* What?

JAMES .*(Who has had enough)* "What?"!! That— that—that *animal!*

SONNY. *(As he sits behind desk and places his feet on it)* Oh, that's Silas Marner. Pam's dog. He always does that when Pam cries. Intuition.

LILLIAN. *(A long, embarrassed pause. Finally* LIL-

LIAN *clears her throat and speaks in a high, social-tea voice, trying to brush off the situation. Lightly)* Well, off to Mexico! Off we go. *(Crosses to* JAMES, *who is upset and puzzled in hall)* I can't begin to tell you how much the children appreciate your kindness, Jimmie. *(Kisses him, ignoring his trance-like attitude)* Clifford and I will write you and if anything should happen—though I can't imagine *what* it could be—Sonny knows where we'll be staying every night. *(Crosses to* SONNY*)* Goodbye, my little boy. You be nice now.

SONNY. Like Pam, you mean?

LILLIAN. *(Kissing him)* And take good care of your sister.

SONNY. Mother—sister can handle herself.

LILLIAN. Clifford.

JAMES. *(Coming out of it)* Did—did—did you hear what she said? *(Then louder as he grows angry and steps into room)* Did you hear what she called me?

SONNY. *I* did, Unc. (JAMES *glares at him)* She said you were young and handsome. Remember?

JAMES. She did not! She said I was a grouchy, stingy old man.

SONNY. *Also* contemptible.

CLIFFORD. *(Shaking* JAMES' *limp hand sadly)* You have all my condolences, Jim. *(Goes to* SONNY*)* You mind your uncle. And *not* the way you mind me. *(Shakes his hand and goes into hall, with a little smile at* CARRIE.*)*

LILLIAN. *(To* JAMES*)* Don't pay any attention to Cliff—he always tries to be so funny. *(Kisses* JAMES *on cheek)* Be good to my dear little children, will you? I—I almost feel like crying—

JAMES. So do I.

LILLIAN. But I shan't!

SONNY. Just before we got here, you told Pop you felt like singing. You said you'd feel like a free woman. And he said he wished he could feel like a free man.

*(*CLIFFORD *goes out front door quickly.)*

LILLIAN. *(Ominously)* I'll speak to your father. *(She marches into hall and out front door.)*

(There is a lengthy pause.)

JAMES. *(Crossing wearily to sofa)* I've decided I'm a weak man.

CARRIE. You don't eat enough.

SONNY. *(Rises and wanders around room; looks at trophies over fireplace)* Did you win these, Unc?

JAMES. *(Wearily as he sits on sofa)* Yes.

SONNY. I can hardly believe it.

JAMES. Carrie—

CARRIE. *(Stepping down)* Yes, Mr. Clark?

JAMES. We'll have a very small lunch. My stomach has that ulcer-feeling again.

SONNY. Carrie—

CARRIE. *(Who has started to go into living room down Left)* Yes?

SONNY. I could eat about half a dozen hamburgers—

CARRIE. *(As she leaves)* Who couldn't?

SONNY. *(Inspecting reducing contraption)* This yours, Unc?

JAMES. *(Going to books on top of radio, regards them sadly, wistfully)* I guess so. *(Picks up book)* This was going to be such a quiet summer.

SONNY. How much'd it set you back?

JAMES. Thirty-three dollars and seventy-two cents.

SONNY. You were robbed. *(He has fitted himself into machine—or has placed reducing strap around him, depending on type of machine used)* What you need's a little exercise—and maybe a few rolls on your stomach. *(Crosses to Left in front of desk)* Want me to show you?

JAMES. No, thanks.

SONNY. Oh, don't be such a goop. Now watch— *(He gets down on floor, lying on his stomach; with his hands he grabs his ankles and starts to rock back and forth on his stomach)* I knew a woman once lost seventeen pounds this way. Why don't you try it?

JAMES. Some other time—maybe. *(Crosses to Center to watch, fascinated.)*

SONNY. It's kinda fun.

(At this point HELEN enters through French doors. With her is LESLIE GARDNER, a man about JAMES' age, wearing golf clothes; he is a ruddy, rugged-looking man with a sly way of speaking. HELEN stops up Right, LESLIE beside her.)

JAMES. Are you sure that will take off weight?

LESLIE. Oh, sure. Nothing better if you have a paunch. *(Slaps stomach)* Not that *I* do.

(SONNY continues to rock, but JAMES, embarrassed, whirls around to face LESLIE and HELEN. LESLIE wears a mocking smile; he has, throughout, a rather irritating, superior attitude.)

JAMES. *(To HELEN)* So you came back.

HELEN. *(As she crosses toward Center, pointing to SONNY, who is still rocking happily)* Did he come in that box?

JAMES. That's my nephew. Sonny—Sonny, this is Miss Russell, my—uh—my secretary. And that other unpleasant-looking creature is Leslie Gardner, who thinks he can teach golf.

LESLIE. Now is that any way to talk to an old friend? And you a politician. *(Crosses to up Left chair.)*

SONNY. Hello! *(He lets go one ankle and as a result his chin hits the floor rather hard)* Ouch! *(Stands up.)*

HELEN. James—you must be nice to Leslie today.

LESLIE. *(Sinking into up Left chair)* For a change.

HELEN. Because he brings you big news. That's why I got over my mad. I ran into Leslie—

LESLIE. You were *looking* for me at the Club. Don't deny it.

HELEN. I was *not!*

LESLIE. Of course you were. *(To JAMES)* You better

watch your step, James. I'll take her right away from you. I've wanted to for some time now.

SONNY. *(Who has wandered up to look more closely at* LESLIE*)* Be careful what you say to him. That's my uncle.

LESLIE. That's your hard luck, kid.

SONNY. Yeah? Well, everybody might as well know right now. I intend to stand up for him and help him in whatever he says. From now on I'm his right hand— even if I do think he's a dope.

JAMES. *(With a false smile)* Thanks. *(Then to* HELEN*)* So you were looking for him, were you?

HELEN. Yes, I was. But only because I wanted to find out what the Nominating Committee had done. And—

JAMES. *(Immediately excited)* Nominating Committee! Oh, Lord, I almost forgot! I've been so—these kids have—all this has— *(Stops; looks at* LESLIE *challengingly)* Well—*what?*

LESLIE. Against my better judgment and against my personal vote—they nominated you.

JAMES. *(Pleased)* They *did?*

LESLIE. *(Meaningfully)* You and Mr. Henry Morgan.

JAMES. *(His cheer fading)* Oh!

HELEN. Yes—I should think—oh! Now you *will* have a fight on your hands.

JAMES. *(Sinking to chair behind desk)* I'm licked.

SONNY. *(Striking him resounding across the back)* Never say die, Unc! (JAMES *winces)* I don't get all this yet, but you're never licked until you say Uncle.

JAMES. *(In a little voice)* Uncle.

SONNY. *(Turning to* HELEN*)* Are you the girl friend?

HELEN. You heard him. I'm his secretary.

SONNY. Yeah—that's what he said. But I've always found you can't trust a man in love. He'll say anything. *(Crosses to* HELEN, *who backs up a step)* Who is this Henry Morgan? Sounds like a pirate to me.

HELEN. He *is* a pirate. He owns everything worth

owning in town, including the newspaper. And he's been running the Country Club for years.

LESLIE. And he doesn't like— *(Points to* JAMES. *Rises)* Well, I have done my job. You have my message. *(Looks at watch)* And I have a pupil coming in fifteen minutes—a golf pupil. Blonde. *(Smiles at* HELEN*)* Any time you want to take up the game, Helen, let me know. I guarantee satisfaction. And fun, too. Especially when I teach you how to hold your club. *(Looks once at* JAMES *and crosses to hall)* So-long, Blackstone! Wait till you see the campaign Morgan pulls. He wants to be President of that club more than he wants more money—and that's plenty! *(With a flip wave of his hand, he exits front door.)*

SONNY. *(Staring after him)* Unc—I've got a feeling that guy doesn't like you.

HELEN. James—aren't you excited? You always said winning the Club Presidency would be the first step to the District Attorney's office.

JAMES. I know. But it looks like I'll miss that step.

HELEN. *(Sitting angrily on sofa)* Oh, you make me tired. With that attitude you're beaten before you start.

SONNY. *(Crossing to* HELEN*)* I like you.

HELEN. Well, thank you.

SONNY. I'm very frank. *(Sits beside her)* Don't you think women like men that way—instead of all that *(Points to* JAMES*)* weazel-guff?

(JEANIE DAY, *a pert sixteen but a trifle shy at first, enters through French doors and comes down Right during following.)*

HELEN. Sonny—I think you're going to be very good for your uncle's morale.

JAMES. Hah!

SONNY. *Good* for it? I'm going to *cure* it. And the first thing on my program is to get him elected— *(His hand is in the air—he sees* JEANIE *for first time. He stops talking, staring.)*

JEANIE. Hello, there!

SONNY. *(Rising)* Well—helloooo! *(Smiling, he steps toward her.)*

HELEN. *(Rising)* Oh, hello, Jeanie— Sonny, this is Jeanie Day. I asked her to drop around to meet you and your sister. By the way, where *is* your sister?

SONNY. Pam's upstairs crying.

HELEN. *(Looking at* JAMES, *who throws up his hands)* Crying? *(She crosses to Left of Center.)*

SONNY. Sure! She does it all the time. *(To* JEANIE*)* All girls do, they say. But I'll bet you're not the type, are you, Jeanie? I can tell by just looking at you. You know, this begins to look like a very interesting summer.

JEANIE. Mister—you've got a line.

SONNY. I'm from New York.

JEANIE. Oh, the boys around here all have lines, too.

SONNY. You're not going steady or anything, are you, Jeanie?

JEANIE. No. Not now.

SONNY. Where do you live?

JEANIE. I'm in the summer camp up the road. There are one hundred and twelve of us.

SONNY. *(Very pleased—taking it big)* One hundred and twelve girls—all in one place? And here I was wondering where they hid the chickadees in this part of the woods! *(Turns and crosses to* JAMES*)* —May I borrow your car?

JAMES. *(Rising)* I'm afraid—that is, my car—well, there's something wrong with it.

SONNY. Oh, that's all right. I'll fix it! *(Goes to take* JEANIE's *hand)* Come on, Jeanie—I'll fix it up and then we'll take a spin down to this haven of playmates and meet the girls. *(He is taking her to hall)* Do they all look like you—I hope? *(Does a little hop in his step)* Whee—I knew it couldn't all be as bad as it looked.

JAMES. Wait— Now listen, Sonny—you—are you sure you know how to repair a car?

SONNY. Relax, Unc. I can fix anything! Let me be useful around here.

JAMES. Well, that *would* be an advantage.

SONNY. *(To* JEANIE *as he leads her into hall and out front door)* You may as well know now, Jeanie, I'm completely and utterly unattached this summer. I just broke it off with three girls. You see, they got too possessive. And also—they had birthdays coming this month—

*(*JEANIE *and* SONNY *are off.* HELEN *looks at* JAMES, *who is staring after them.)*

JAMES. *(Worried)* Aren't they—don't they seem young to you
HELEN. *(With a light laugh)* James—you are getting old.
JAMES. I feel about a hundred and eighty right this minute. *(Appealing)* Helen—what have I let myself in for?
HELEN. I hold to my original contention: it'll be good for you!
JAMES. Helen—stick by me.
HELEN. Good ole Helen! *(Crosses to desk and picks up telephone book)* Sure— I think we ought to give the kids a party, get them acquainted. I'll make some telephone calls.
JAMES. They *would* have to nominate Morgan! That was probably Leslie Gardner's doings.
HELEN. Now don't start attacking Leslie.
JAMES. Oh, I know how you feel about him.
HELEN. I didn't say anything about—
JAMES. You made that clear. Even that child caught it. Well, why don't you go play golf with him? *(He is pacing—getting himself worked up)* Go on—go play golf. And let him hold your hand. And teach you how to swing the clubs and yell "Fore." I can do that. *(Loud)* Fore! There. *(Louder)* Fore!
HELEN. James, what's come over you?
CARRIE. *(Enters from living room)* Did you want me?
JAMES. You get out of here!

CARRIE. *(Jumping and turning)* I thought I heard someone yelling—

JAMES. *(At her retreating back—loud) Fore!*

CARRIE. *(Turns)* Don't you start calling me names! *(She exits.)*

HELEN. James—control yourself. This is only the beginning.

(There is a KNOCK at the front door. CARRIE sticks her head in, unsure whether she should answer it.)

JAMES. *(Loud)* I told you to get out of here! I'll go! *(Crosses to hall and opens door.)*

(HELEN sits at desk and jots down telephone numbers. VOICES can be heard.)

MR. MORGAN. *(Off)* Good morning, James. *(He appears)* Practising your golf, were you?

(MR. MORGAN is a portly, hearty man—a pillar of the community and aware of it. He tries to be friendly and this results in a certain type of almost-insincere glad-handing which, after a while, could be annoying. He is followed by HARRIET MORGAN, his daughter, age seventeen. HARRIET is a tall, willowy girl, conscious of her wealth and her charm. Under different circumstances, she could have been a rather appealing girl; but her position and her father's attitudes have turned her into something of a snob.)

HARRIET. We could hear you all the way from the road, Mr. Clark.

JAMES. I—I had a little trouble with my—with my throat. A frog caught in it.

MORGAN. *(Coming down into room)* Sounded more like a hippopotamus. *(He likes his little joke and roars at it.* HELEN *rises and turns)* —Not bad, that. Good joke, eh? Hippopotamus!

(Goes off into another roar of laughter until HARRIET *steps from hall and stops him.)*

HARRIET. Daddy!
MORGAN. Eh? Oh, sorry. Well, it *was* funny. No sense of humor—that's what's the matter with everyone. (JAMES *crosses to Center and waits; he gestures to the sofa for* MR. MORGAN*) —*Thanks, James. *(Sits.)*
JAMES. You know my—my secretary, don't you, Mr. Morgan?
MORGAN. Certainly do. How do you do, Miss Russell? Very pretty. How do you manage to look so pretty all the time? You know my daughter, Harriet—

(There is a general exchange of "How-do-you-do's" while HARRIET *wanders to up Right, looking over the room, and* JAMES *stands waiting to see what this is all about.)*

JAMES. Would you like some—some lemoñade, Mr. Morgan? Hot day and—
MORGAN. No, no, no. No time for that. *(Turns)* Harriet—where's Bill?
HARRIET. He stopped to watch the garageman repair Mr. Clark's car. *(Looking out French doors)* Here he comes. *(Calls out)* Bill.
MORGAN. That young man can't keep his mind on one thing at a time. Like all young people today. You wouldn't know about that, James, but believe me, *I* do.
HELEN. James is learning.

*(*BILL HENLY *enters through French doors.* HARRIET *leads him down to Center for introductions.* BILL *is an impressive-looking, handsome boy of eighteen, with a quiet, assured manner and an easy smile.)*

HARRIET. Miss Russell—this is Bill Henly. And Mr. Clark—Bill Henly.
JAMES. How do you do?

HELEN. Hello, Bill!

BILL. Hullo!

(HARRIET *takes his arm possessively.*)

MORGAN. Now—what I dropped by to see you about, James, is simply this: I don't mean to mince words. I want to congratulate you on your nomination. And also I want to tell you that—as your opponent—I'm prepared to give you the battle of your life! All in good fun, of course. All in the very best of good fun! *(Laughs jovially, loudly.)*

JAMES. *(Straightening)* I think I can safely say—I *will* safely say—the same goes for me.

HELEN. *(Listlessly)* Hurrah, hurray!

(JAMES *flashes her a look.*)

MORGAN. And may the best man win! *(Rises and shakes* JAMES' *hand heartily.)*

BILL. Mr. Clark—

JAMES. Yes, Bill?

BILL. Do you have an upstairs maid?

JAMES. Maid? Why, no, I—

BILL. Because as I came in, someone upstairs pulled back the curtains and looked down and— *(With an abashed smile)* well, she was so—so good-looking—I just wondered.

MORGAN. Good-looking? A *maid* good-looking?

BILL. That's possible, Mr. Morgan.

HARRIET. Bill! Bill Henly—what are you up to now?

BILL. I'm not up to anything. But if I should meet a maid and she was good-looking, I'd think she was as good as I am—or you are—that's all. That's all.

MORGAN. *(To* JAMES) See—that's what the world's coming to. *(Shakes hands again)* Well, I came to say what I said and I said it.

HELEN. *(Unable to control herself)* And are you glad?

MORGAN. *(Roaring with laughter)* Glad?—That's

good. *(To* JAMES*)* She's a funny one, James. *(Crossing to* HELEN*)* You ever get tired of working for him, Miss Russell, you look me up at my newspaper office— or at the bank. I'm sure we could find a place for a bright young lady like you.

HELEN. Mr. Morgan—you may be able to use your newspaper and your bank and your tremendous influence to win the election—but my heart belongs to Daddy. *(Points to* JAMES*.)*

MORGAN. That sounds insulting.

JAMES. She didn't mean to be— Did you, Helen? Miss Russell? (HELEN *doesn't answer)* Oh, Miss Russell—

HELEN. *(Flatly)* I didn't mean to be insulting.

HARRIET. *(Who has been talking to* BILL *in whispers upstage)* Sometimes I don't understand you at all— you and your ideas!

BILL. Not now, Harriet. Not here.

SONNY. *(His clothes smeared with grease, enters at front door. Briskly)* It's your carburetor, Unc. *(In hall)* Anybody got a hairpin?

JAMES. *(Astounded) Hairpin?!*

SONNY. Don't tell me you've never seen a hairpin?!

HELEN. Here— *(Removes one from hair and gives it to him.)*

SONNY. Thanks, Miss Russell. I knew I could depend on you. *(Turns and exits with hairpin.)*

MORGAN. That's what I mean—even the repairmen don't know their place these days!

JAMES. That was no repairman. It was my nephew —and I hope he knows what he's doing.

MORGAN. Your nephew?

JAMES. Yes, my niece and nephew are visiting me for the summer. She's upstairs. *(Confidentially)* And to tell you the truth, she's a bit upset about life today. She's up there crying and I—I don't know what to do about it.

BILL. *(Stepping down)* Maybe I could do something about it. I'd like to meet her.

JAMES. Oh, no, no, no. She's—well, as I said, crying

and weeping and her hair's all down over her face probably—

HARRIET. *(Stepping down to* BILL*)* Why do *you* want to meet her?

JAMES. And she probably looks a wreck. She wouldn't want to meet—

(He turns to hallway to find PAMELA *standing there. She is in fine fettle and looks even prettier than when we first met her. She is smiling as she listens.)*

PAMELA. Hello—

JAMES. Pamela!

PAMELA. You're always so considerate, Uncle Jimmie. *(Goes to him and takes his arm charmingly)* Isn't he wonderful? Now introduce me to all these very nice— *(She looks at* BILL, *who smiles back)* people, won't you?

JAMES. Uh—yes, of course. This is my niece, Pamela—Miss Morgan, Miss Russell, Mr. Morgan—

(He skips BILL; *but* PAMELA *hasn't taken her eyes from him.)*

BILL. I'm Bill Henly.

PAMELA. I'm Pam.

BILL. Hello!

PAMELA. Hello!

(A pause.)

HARRIET. I'm Harriet Morgan— *(Steps to* PAMELA*)* and I say be careful.

PAMELA. I'm Pamela Young—and I don't know *what* you mean.

(A moment while the TWO GIRLS *size each other up.)*

JAMES. *(Wanting to smooth it over)* Oh, Miss Morgan—we're having a party for Pamela and her brother. Perhaps you and Mr. Henly here would like to come. On—on—

HELEN. Saturday.

JAMES. That's it—on Saturday.

BILL. *(Promptly, still looking at* PAMELA*)* I'd like to.

HARRIET. I'm afraid I have other plans for Saturday. *(Her voice belies her word)* Sorry.

PAMELA. Then perhaps Bill would enjoy coming—alone.

BILL. Well, I—

HARRIET. My plans are *with* Bill.

PAMELA. Maybe Bill has some independent plans—now.

BILL. Well, I—

HARRIET. *(Definitely)* He has *not*.

PAMELA. Bill—?

BILL. No, you see—as a matter of fact—I do have a date with Harriet.

HARRIET. *Every* Saturday—if you know what I mean.

PAMELA. *(As she crosses to sit on sofa, smiling)* Some Friday, then—when you're free.

HARRIET. Daddy! Daddy, listen to that girl!

MORGAN. I hear her. *(Crosses to* PAMELA*)* Where do you come from, young lady?

PAMELA. New York. Where do *you* come from?

MORGAN. Never mind that. All I can say is that in this community, we respect other people's property.

PAMELA. In New York we don't consider a *person* property.

BILL. No, sir—I resent being called property.

HARRIET. Bill!

JAMES. Now—uh—let's just be calm about this. No need to—

MORGAN. *(Irascibly—to* JAMES*) You* stay out of it. She's your niece.

JAMES. I intend to.

PAMELA. Does everyone here take orders from Mr.

Morgan? And Mr. Morgan's daughter? *(To* BILL*)* Do they, Bill?

BILL. Well—

PAMELA. I'd be ashamed.

MORGAN. Now see here—I didn't come here to be insulted.

PAMELA. Why *did* you come here?

JAMES. Now Pam—

PAMELA. And what are you afraid of, Uncle Jimmie? I thought you were going to be District Attorney.

MORGAN. District Attorney? *(Turns to* JAMES*)* So that's what you've got your eye on, is it? Well, let me tell you—all of you—if my paper decides you'll be District Attorney, you'll be it. And if my paper—meaning me—decides against you—

PAMELA. Is that what they call freedom of the press?

JAMES. Pam, please—

MORGAN. *(Placing hat on head)* And right now my paper is definitely undecided. Harriet. Bill. Come on— *(Starts for hall.)*

JAMES. Now just a minute, Mr. Morgan. Pam didn't mean—

MORGAN. *(Thinking of something)* And furthermore —when my daughter rides in that parade in our float, as the symbol of Truth and Honesty—which is me— every single member of the Club will vote for me.

PAMELA. What float?

JAMES. Never mind. It's just a parade we have every year—just before the election. And each nominee has a float—

PAMELA. Parade? *(Rises—excited)* I love parades. May I ride your float, Uncle Jimmie?

JAMES. No. Miss Russell is riding my float.

MORGAN. I came here in the spirit of friendship and—

HELEN. You did *not*, Mr. Morgan. You came here to tell James you were going to walk off with the election.

PAMELA. And you won't!

HARRIET. We'll see about that. *(Crosses to hall)* Bill, are you coming?

PAMELA. "Bill, are you coming?" What are you, anyway? A sheep-dog?

BILL. Not yet, Harriet. *(Crosses to PAMELA)* Would you like to go dancing with this "piece of property" on Friday night, Miss Young?

PAMELA. I'd love it, Mr. Henly.

HARRIET. Father—did you hear that?

MORGAN. I heard it. And I've heard enough.

(From outside there is an EXPLOSION—sound of backfire. MORGAN jumps. JAMES rushes to window. HELEN rises.)

JAMES. Now what—?

HARRIET. Father!

MORGAN. I'm getting out of here!

SONNY. *(Smeared with grease from head to foot this time, appears excitedly in front doorway and addresses room from hall)* Now don't get excited, anyone. It was just a backfire. Something went wrong with a gasket— or something.   *(WARN Curtain.)*

PAMELA. Sonny! Sonny, what are you doing?

JAMES. He said he was repairing my car.

PAMELA. *(With a little shriek)* Oh, no! Uncle Jimmie—he can't repair anything. Don't let him *touch* it. He can never get anything back together!

SONNY. Jeanie's underneath it now. She touched something and then—wowie! But don't worry.

PAMELA. You stay in here, Sonny. I want you to help me with something—a campaign to win the elections for Uncle Jimmie.

SONNY. Not now, Pam. Jeanie's under the car and— *(He starts for door, but stops when we hear another EXPLOSION, this time much louder, off stage)* Too late.

JAMES. No!

CARRIE. *(Enters from living room)* I didn't fix lunch for this many people.

PAMELA. *(Crossing to desk—to* HELEN*)* I'll take over the whole campaign. Uncle Jimmie—you've practically won already!

JEANIE. *(Enters front door; she is grease from head to foot. Near tears—accusingly to* SONNY*)* You didn't tell me it would do *that!*

MORGAN. I'm getting out of this house! *(Rushes out front door, slamming hat on head.)*

(HARRIET *and* BILL *follow* MR. MORGAN, BILL *looking back at* PAMELA, *and the Curtain begins to fall.)*

JEANIE. And look at me! Sonny Young—I ought to sue you or something!

JAMES. *(Sinking to chair at Left)* Lillian. *(Weakly)* Lillian—take them away.

(HELEN *is comforting him.* BILL *and* HARRIET *are leaving.* PAMELA *is clearing off the desk and taking cover off typewriter.* SONNY *is running out French doors, with* JEANIE *after him. Outside the* DOG *has begun to bark.* CARRIE *is speaking.)*

CARRIE. Lunch is served.

But The Curtain Has Fallen.

ACT TWO

SCENE I

SCENE: *The same.*

TIME: *The following Saturday evening, around seven-thirty.*

AT RISE: *The room has undergone some change—some drastic change. No longer is it the quiet, dignified study. Instead it is a Campaign Room. A card-table has been set up, up Center, in front of fireplace; on it is* PAMELA'S *portable typewriter. Over the mantel—and decorating the walls—are posters, with large, vivid painted pictures and such slogans as: "Clark for President" and "A Great Country Club Needs a Great Leader" and "Stay Honest—Elect Honesty" and "Stay Young With Clark." Also scattered around the room are tennis rackets, golf clubs, and sweaters, sneakers, and so forth. The two fencing foils are lying on the sofa. Records are lying all over the radio-phonograph; and it is playing—loud boogie-woogie.*

PAMELA, *wearing shorts or slacks, sits at typewriter on card-table and* SONNY, *wearing a brilliant sports-shirt and spotty slacks, sits at typewriter on desk. For a long moment both type industriously;* PAMELA *goes fairly fast, but* SONNY *picks and strikes, taking a rather long time and making much of finding each letter.* SONNY *has sandwiches and fruit beside typewriter on desk; and as he works, he eats.*

After a long moment—while the audience takes in the changed set and SONNY *has much trouble with the keys:*

43

SONNY. How do you spell stupendous?

PAMELA *(Not looking up)* S-t-o-o-o-p·e-n-d-o-u-s.

SONNY. *(Typing it out)* S-t-c o-p-e-n-d-o-u-s. Thanks.

(They BOTH *type again.)*

PAMELA. Where's Uncle Jimmie?

SONNY. Taking a bath. He's awfully worried about this party tonight. And he's been complaining all week about the bathtub. He says I monopolize it. *(Thinks)* Say—that's a good angle. Henry Morgan is a monopolist. That's an idea for a slogan. "Don't Elect a Monopolist."

PAMELA. Write it down. (SONNY *does)* —Uncle Jimmie's right, Sonny. You *have* been living in the bathtub.

SONNY. How else can a guy keep cool?—You know, you don't seem very girlishly thrilled about this party tonight.

PAMELA. Why should I? *(Dreamily)* No one's coming I care about.

SONNY. Yeah—I know who you mean. Did you have a good time at the dance last night?

PAMELA. Heavenly!

SONNY. "Heavenly." Pam—you haven't got a chance. Against a gal like Harriet Morgan—and all that money.

PAMELA. Bill Henly doesn't care a fig about money!

SONNY. Is that what he fed you? In the moonlight, I suppose—with a kiss or two thrown in. Well, I always say don't trust a man who says he doesn't care about money. Either he's a liar—and you don't want a liar. Or he's a dope—and you don't want a dope, either. *(Blithely)* I'd say you were in an impossible situation.

PAMELA. Aw, shut up.

SONNY. *(Cordially)* Sure. *(He goes back to his typing. Then:)* Where is he tonight, by the way?

PAMELA. He has a date with Harriet—the pirate's daughter.

SONNY. While poor Jeffrey languishes around New York with your palsy-walsies. Poor girl.

PAMELA. I said shut up.

CARRIE. *(Enters from living room; stands looking at the two of them)* I thought there was to be a party around here this evening. *(No answer)* Why aren't you two ready? *(No answer)* I've been meaning to tell you —I think your uncle would have a better chance of winning this election if it weren't for your help. *(No answer: just the clatter of typewriters)* I came in to tell you about your dog. *(She moves toward PAMELA)* Your *dog! (Louder)* He won't eat the dog food!

PAMELA. *(Immediately aroused and rising)* Dog food!? Have you been trying to feed my poor little doggie *dog food? (Crosses to living room door)* What do you think he is? *(Exits in a huff.)*

CARRIE. *(Staring after her)* I don't know. A dog, isn't he?

SONNY. *(Unperturbed)* How do you spell colossal?

CARRIE. *(Spelling with no hesitation)* K-o-l-l-a-s-s-o-l.

SONNY. *(Typing)* Thanks.

CARRIE. Anyone knows that.

(There is a KNOCK at the front door. CARRIE goes into hall and opens door. It is TONY, the express-man, again; this time he has two large packages.)

TONY. More packages for Pamela Young.

CARRIE. *(Disgusted)* Bring them in. *(Steps into room.)*

TONY. *(Entering and placing packages at Center)* This makes the fifth time I've been out here today. *(Hands book to CARRIE)* Who is this Pamela Young? The way I figure it, owning all this junk, she must be moving in. How old is she?

SONNY. *(Quickly)* About your age.

(CARRIE signs book.)

Tony. *(Pleased)* She *is?* Say, I had a fight with my girl friend and this might work out pretty fine. *(To* Carrie*)* Is she pretty?

Carrie. Get out of here.

Tony. Okay, lady! *(Takes book)* I just had an idea —but people are always so funny. Take this Pamela Young—a lady about my age—now, here she is, moving in out here in the country—and I could maybe keep her company, show her the town. But no—she's rich and I'm just a delivery-man. *(Shrugs)* Goes to show.

Sonny. Look, Mister—Miss Young isn't like that at all. She's giving a party here this evening. Why don't you come back and meet her? Who knows?

Tony. *(Beaming)* Who knows? You said it! Who knows?

Carrie. *(To* Sonny*)* What are you up to?

Sonny. *(To* Tony*)* How do you spell spectacular?

Tony. *(Promptly)* S-p-e-c-k-t-a-c-k-u-l-a-r. *(Goes out front door, very happy)* I'll be back—if no more packages come in!

Carrie. *(Starting for living room again)* Anyone knows how to spell spectacular. Where did you go to school? *(Exits.)*

(Sonny *types for a moment; then he gets up and picks up saxophone from up Left chair and crosses to sofa. He stretches out, with one foot over the back of sofa, and starts to play—not very well, perhaps.* James, *very flustered and looking more and more like a baffled puppy, comes downstairs and into hall, stops; seeing* Sonny, *his eyes go heavenward in a silent prayer—perhaps for aid to hold his temper.)*

James. Sonny! (Sonny *waves one hand cheerily)* Look at this room! Look at it. *(Crosses to living room door; throws it open)* Carrie! Carrie! *(Closes door and faces room)* We can't have people here with the room in this shape. *(Crosses toward* Sonny*)* And you're not even dressed. *(Goes to turn off radio.)*

SONNY. I know. *(Sits up)* Unc—I been thinking.

JAMES. *(Looks at walls and posters)* No! Who did that? Who—

SONNY. Those are for you, Unc. Aren't they super?

JAMES. Super? They're undignified and—

SONNY. Unc—you know what's the matter with you? You don't know how to relax and you can't enjoy any thing. If it's the last thing I do this summer, I'm going to teach you how to have a good time.

JAMES. *(Grimly)* It *might* be the last thing you do—

CARRIE. *(Enters from living room)* Pamela's feeding the dog roast pork.

SONNY. Does he like it?

CARRIE. That roast pork is for tomorrow's dinner!

JAMES. Carrie—look at this place! How can we have guests with the house in this shape?

CARRIE. Mr. Clark—

SONNY. Relax, Unc. Like this, see— *(He demonstrates on sofa)* I'm completely relaxed.

JAMES. That's your job, Carrie—keeping some order around here.

CARRIE. Mr. Clark, you listen to me. What you need is a staff of twenty servants and ten footmen—and maybe a slave or two. I been trying to cook meals big enough to feed the whole Navy—and salads on the side for your stomach. I've been scrubbing out bathtubs and on my knees in the kitchen with a brush. I've been trying to answer the door sixty times a day and losing thirty pounds answering the telephone— In short, Mr. Clark—I'm going crazy. And now if you start—

JAMES. *(Starts picking up sweaters, etc.)* I'm sorry, Carrie—

CARRIE. *(Loftily)* Sorry isn't enough! *(Turns and goes into living room again.)*

JAMES. *(Staring after her)* Now what's the matter with *her?*

SONNY. Relax, Unc. Relax.

JAMES. *(Crossing to face SONNY)* Listen, Sonny— if you say that to me once more—just *once* more—

SONNY. You're only thirty-five. When you're fifty, you'll look seventy.

JAMES. If there aren't some reforms around here, I won't live to be fifty.

PAMELA. *(Enters from living room)* The nerve of that woman! *(Sees* JAMES*)* Oh, hello, Uncle Jimmie! Isn't everything going beautifully? You're practically *in. (Goes to up Center and starts taking down card table in slow, unhappy movements.)*

JAMES. Pam—you aren't ready yet, either!

PAMELA. No.

JAMES. *(Crossing to her)* What's the matter, Pam? Is there anything I can— I mean—

PAMELA. Why, bless your heart. You *can* be nice, can't you?

JAMES. *(Flustered, starts to round up the odds and ends spread around the room)* I haven't had a chance to be nice. It cost forty-five dollars to have my car repaired. The dog tore up my garden. These posters and all this advertising is going to cost me the Country Club election—and the Country Club election is going to cost me the District Attorney's office! What have I got to be nice about? *(By now his arms are loaded and he stands near hall door.)*

PAMELA. Uncle Jimmie—you can't lose the election. You don't understand. Sonny made a deal with Leslie Gardner—

JAMES. Leslie Gardner—he'd like to see me lose!

SONNY. Sure, but not after I got finished talking with him.

PAMELA. I should say not! Why, Leslie's a dear. He snitched a complete membership list for us—

SONNY. Sure—and we're writing letters to everyone telling them what a great guy you are—

JAMES. No—

PAMELA. And what a heel Mr. Morgan is—

JAMES. *(Much louder—hopelessly)* No! Listen, kids —that's unethical. That sort of thing will only lead to— Where are those letters?

SONNY. *(Blandly)* You'll get one tomorrow, Unc. Your name was on the list.

JAMES. Now you two kids listen to me. You're fired. My campaign is over. I'm going to cede the election to Mr. Morgan and forget about it.

SONNY. *(Leaping up)* Unc—you can't.

PAMELA. *(Crossing to* JAMES *at up Left)* Don't be an imbecile—

JAMES. And furthermore, if either one of you— *(He gets what* PAMELA *has said)* I am *not* an imbecile!

PAMELA. We won't let you throw away all our work—

SONNY. And think of the girls at Camp Tuckahoe!

JAMES. There simply has to be some sort of understanding around this house until— *(He gets what* SONNY *has said)* What have the girls at Camp Tuckahoe got to do with it?

SONNY. They're all on your side, Unc. In fact, they're helping me design the float for the parade next Saturday. And they painted these posters.

PAMELA. And that's not all—they're going to ride in front of the float—singing their Camp songs. *(Bursts into song, illustrating)* "On the shores of Lake Tuckahoe, in the hills of Somerset—"

SONNY. *(Grabbing saxophone, accompanies)* People will hear them for miles.

JAMES. *(Stopping them)* I said no, and I mean no! That's final and irrevocable! *(Turns and starts up stairs.)*

PAMELA. *(Crosses to sit behind desk)* Okay! Then you'll never be District Attorney.

JAMES. I said final and I mean— *(He stops, thinks a moment; then slowly, while* SONNY *pretends interest in saxophone and* PAMELA *refuses to turn her head,* JAMES *comes into room again. Then in a little voice)* Well, it may not be *completely* final. But please, kids—please—let's keep it—*dignified.* Sonny? Pamela? *Will* you?

SONNY. Dignity's our second name, Unc.

PAMELA. We promise, Unc.

JAMES. Very well, then. *(Turns to go into hall.)*

SONNY. By the way, Unc—do you know where we can hire a mule? I want to ride it around town playing my saxophone until I get a crowd together. Then I tell them all about you and Mr. Morgan—

JAMES. *(With a cry of pain as he stomps up the stairs)* A mule? I'm ruined, I'm ruined, *I'm ruined—!!*

PAMELA. Can't you learn to keep your big mouth shut?

SONNY. Can I help it if I'm imaginative?

(During the following PAMELA and SONNY place card table against wall and gather up the remaining odds and ends around room. However, the posters remain.)

PAMELA. I don't know why I do this—when I'm so miserable I could spit.

SONNY. That's the trouble with women—they always take love so seriously. Now take men—do we? No. We use our heads to keep our hearts in hand.

PAMELA. I don't want any of your crazy advice.

SONNY. Okay— Only look at me. Am I ever unhappy over some slick chick? No. Girls are so dumb you can play one off against the other. Then you can't lose. That's probably what Bill's doing with you and Harriet.

PAMELA. Bill is not! He's not like you.

SONNY. Okay— Only his heart's not all torn up and tramped on—you can bet that right now he's telling Harriet exactly what he told you last night.

PAMELA. *(Thoughtfully)* Do you think so?

SONNY. Makes sense—to a man.

PAMELA. *(Angry)* I don't believe you! *(Starts for hall.)*

SONNY. *(Cynically, looking after her)* No? Then what are you so sore about?

PAMELA. I'm not sore. But I hope I never see Bill Henly again as long as I live! *(Goes up stairs and off.)*

(As PAMELA goes up, the front door opens and HELEN enters. She is dressed for the party in an attractive evening gown with a light cape thrown over her shoulders. Seeing her, SONNY whistles.)

HELEN. What are you doing to Pamela now?

SONNY. Miss Russell, you're swoonsational! My uncle's really a lunkhead.

HELEN. *(Stepping into room)* Has anyone come yet? And don't talk about your uncle that way.

SONNY. *(Going to sofa and pointing to it)* Sit down, Miss Russell. I got something on my mind.

HELEN. I'd think you were sick if you didn't. *(Goes and sits.)*

SONNY. I was just talking it over with Pamela, and now I'm convinced. Women—excuse me, Miss Russell—but women don't use their heads. They get all mixed up with their emotions. You follow me?

HELEN. Vaguely, Sonny. Hadn't we better check up on the refreshments?

SONNY. *(Sitting beside her—earnestly)* Not now. Listen. I want to make a confession. Most men are just like that too. You get me? Except for exceptional men, like me—

HELEN. No, I don't follow you.

SONNY. What I'm getting at is this. You wait till Uncle James walks into this room and sees you in that dress. What will he do? Nothing. What will he say? Nothing. Get me?

HELEN. Your uncle has a lot on his mind.

SONNY. Don't we all? But look—I'm trying to say I know a way you could pop his eyes open and make him notice you.

HELEN. Sonny—I for one will not fall for any of your hair-brained schemes.

SONNY. This isn't a scheme. Are you trying to hurt my feelings? This is plain common sense—psychology, you might say— The only way to bring Unc to life and make him realize what a prize package you are is to make him jealous.

HELEN. And how do you propose I do that?

SONNY. You know Leslie Gardner, don't you? Sure. Well, I'm here to tell you—strictly between us—that guy's gone crackers about you.

HELEN. I beg your pardon?

SONNY. Don't you understand English? He's goof about you, gone, socked in the solar-plexus, shot in the arm. And when he gets here tonight—

HELEN. But he's not coming tonight.

SONNY. I invited him. You see, I believe in tit for tat—get me? And Mr. Gardner did me a favor this week, so I'm doing him a favor now. When he comes, what I want you to do is to go out with him—leave Uncle flat. It'll open the old boy's eyes.

HELEN. I wouldn't think of doing such a thing, Sonny. You better get hold of that imagination of yours.

(There is a KNOCK at the front door. SONNY crosses to windows, looks out; then he turns to HELEN and whispers loudly)

SONNY. It's Jeanie. Now you watch. She's got a coupla gals with her. And Jeanie's already begun to feel my charm, see? But she's sore at me—said she wouldn't even speak to me. Now you watch what happens when you use your old beano. *(Crosses to hall and opens door.)*

(JEANIE enters, followed by BETSY HARRISON, an athletic girl of fifteen with a deep voice and a positive manner, and ESTHER HAMILTON, a gushy feminine type, the same age. All three are dressed for the party. JEANIE ignores SONNY and goes directly to HELEN at sofa; the other TWO GIRLS follow, and SONNY, with a smile, moves down Left, watching.)

JEANIE. Miss Russell—I want you to meet my friend, Betsy Harrison, who's the champion swimmer, tennis-player and wrestler at Camp; and this is Esther Hamilton.

ESTHER. I can't even swim.

HELEN. How do you do, girls? I think you're the first to arrive. Make yourselves at home— Jeanie, aren't you going to introduce your friends to Sonny?

JEANIE. *(Looking around the room, her eyes going right by* SONNY*)* Oh—is there someone else here? I don't see a soul.

(HELEN *represses a smile.)*

SONNY. Oh, that's all right. Jeanie can't see me.

JEANIE. *(As she crosses to down Right)* Humph!

SONNY. *(Crossing to the other* TWO GIRLS*)* Hiya, Betsy? How'd you like to go swimming with me tomorrow?

BETSY. Well, I don't know. Are you good?

SONNY. You can teach me.

BETSY. That might be nice.

SONNY. *(Turning to* ESTHER*)* I'm Sonny, Esther. Will you have the first dance of the evening with me?

ESTHER. I'd love to, Sonny.

SONNY. *(Taking* BOTH GIRLS *by hand, leads them to Left)* I think we three will get along like oldtimers, don't you? I been wanting to meet the other girls at the camp, but Jeanie's so jealous she wouldn't take me up to see all of you.

JEANIE. *(Unable to control herself)* That's a 1—

(SONNY *turns to her. She shuts up and turns away.)*

SONNY. *(Innocently)* Did someone say something?

ESTHER. *(Taking* SONNY's *hand again—with a little giggle)* I didn't hear a thing.

SONNY. I guess I didn't, either. *(Turns back to* GIRLS*)* Boy, I had no idea there were tomatoes as pretty as you two around these parts. Makes me feel at home. I come from New York, you know. But you gals have it all over those New York chicks. Want to hear me play the saxophone?

ESTHER. Oh—do you play the sax?

BETSY. I'd rather fence. *(Crosses to fireplace and gets fencing foils)* Here. *(Shoves one into* SONNY'S *hand.)*

SONNY. No, I—

BETSY. *(Shouting)* On guard!

(She attacks with foil, backing SONNY *around the room; he protects himself as best he can. The attack becomes loud and fast.)*

SONNY. Betsy, I can't—I never—

BETSY. Keep it up, Sonny! There, I'm wide open. Touché. Touché. *(She lunges and whacks him across the leg flatly.)*

SONNY. Owww—

BETSY. *(Tossing foil to up Left chair)* You're no good. It's no fun unless you can fence.

ESTHER. Betsy, I think you're awful. *(Goes to* SONNY*)* Did she hurt you, Sonny?

SONNY. Just my pride. (JEANIE *laughs.* SONNY *turns on her)* What are you giggling at?

JEANIE. *(Sweetly—to* HELEN*)* Did you hear someone say something?

HELEN. Not a word. *(She is laughing, as* JEANIE *sits beside her.)*

JEANIE. Boys always think they can make you jealous if they lift an eye at another girl—as though they were the only boys for miles around.

(There is another KNOCK at front door. HELEN *rises and goes.* SONNY *gets saxophone and sits behind desk, playing softly, with* ESTHER *and* BETSY *grouped around him.* HELEN *opens door. It is* TUBBY PITTS, *a well-padded boy of seventeen with a bright face and a slightly high voice. He is naive, friendly, open-eyed. He smiles at* HELEN.*)*

HELEN. Come in.

TUBBY. Thanks. *(Steps into hall)* I'm Tubby Pitts.

HELEN. I'm Helen Russell.

TUBBY. How do you do? I have a message for Pam Young. From Bill Henly.

HELEN. I'll call her. *(Calls up stairs)* Pam! Pam, there's a boy down here to see you.

PAMELA. *(Off—upstairs)* I'll be right down.

HELEN. *(Taking TUBBY's hand, leads him across to JEANIE on sofa)* Tubby—this is Jeanie Day. We're getting ready for a party here. And I think you and Jeanie should be good friends.

JEANIE. Hello, Tubby!

TUBBY. Hello—

(The saxophone music stops, as SONNY watches from across the room.)

JEANIE. Maybe you'll stay for our party, Tubby.

TUBBY. Gee—I'd be mighty pleased. I haven't been to a party since—let's see—Thursday night. *(Thinks)* —Did I go to a party last night? No. No, it was Thursday. I love parties. *(Sits beside JEANIE.)*

JEANIE. We'd love to have you.

SONNY. *(Standing up)* Say— *(Steps toward Center)* Say—whose party *is* this? You can't do that!

JEANIE. *(To TUBBY, as she takes his hand)* Did you say you had a message for Pamela?

SONNY. Did you hear me?

TUBBY. *(Embarrassed)* Uh—I think someone's talking to you, Jeanie.

SONNY. *(Another step)* You're darned right I am!

JEANIE. *(Perking up)* I didn't hear a thing, Tubby.

SONNY. Hey! *(Very loud)* Stop that foolishness!

TUBBY. *(Looking from SONNY to JEANIE)* I—I—I feel sure someone said something—

JEANIE. You must be mistaken.

TUBBY. Oh! *(Bewildered, he looks from SONNY to JEANIE again, his eyes wide)* Okay!

SONNY. Who do you think you're kidding?

JEANIE. Maybe you'd like to have the first dance with me, Tubby?

TUBBY. I'd be mighty pleased, Jeanie. I love dancing.

SONNY. *(Angry beyond words now, as* HELEN *represses her laughter up stage)* Oh, no, you don't—! I have the first dance and every other dance, too!

ESTHER. *(Stepping up behind* SONNY*)* But Sonny—you and I have the first dance. Remember?

SONNY. *Jeanie, do you hear me?*

TUBBY. *(To* JEANIE*)* I'm *sure* someone is addressing you.

JEANIE. *(Ignoring* SONNY*)* Maybe we ought to go outside a while, Tubby. *(Rises)* It's getting awfully noisy in here. *(Takes* TUBBY'S *hand and he rises, too)* Come on—

TUBBY. I'd be mighty pleased.

(JEANIE *and* TUBBY *start up Right.)*

SONNY. *(Stepping in and taking* TUBBY'S *shoulder and swinging him around)* Say, you. I got a good notion to punch you in the nose.

TUBBY. *(Turning to* JEANIE*)* Don't tell me you didn't hear *that?*

SONNY. Who do you think you are anyway?

TUBBY. My name's Tubby Pitts. I came here to deliver a message for Bill Henly to Pamela Young. But if you want to punch me in the nose, I think we'd better go outside, because I don't want you to break anything in this nice house when you fall.

(*A moment's pause.* SONNY *looks at* TUBBY, *scratches his head once, ruffles his hair, and turns away.)*

SONNY. Well, I'm woofed! *(Turns and goes to Left.)*

HELEN. *(Crossing to* SONNY*)* Sonny—I think your idea was a good one. About jealousy, I mean. I may try it on to see how it fits.

PAMELA. *(Comes down the stairs and pauses in hall. She is gowned for the party and is very excited)* Who is it? *(Pauses on step)* Has Bill come?

TUBBY. *(Crossing to* PAMELA*)* You must be Pam. I'm Tubby Pitts. Bill Henly asked me to come and take care of you this evening.

PAMELA. "Take care of me?"

TUBBY. He kind of wants me to watch over you so none of the wolves can get near you. I'll be mighty pleased.

PAMELA. "Watch over me—?" I never heard anything so insulting in my whole life. Watch over me while he's out dancing with Harriet Morgan!

TUBBY. Bill and I are old pals. I'll do anything for Bill—even things I don't like to do.

PAMELA. *(Bitterly)* Thanks.

TUBBY. *(Quickly)* But that certainly doesn't apply to this. I'll be mighty honored.

PAMELA. Tubby—you're sweet.

JEANIE. *(Stepping in)* He is not! *(To* PAMELA*)* I saw him first.

SONNY. *(Laughing)* Nice work, Sis.

JEANIE. *(Across to* SONNY*)* You stay out of this!

(LESLIE GARDNER, *wearing a dinner suit, enters at French doors; leans in them during the following.)*

SONNY. *(To* JEANIE*)* I thought you weren't talking to me.

JEANIE. I'm not.

TUBBY. Bill said to say he'd try to drop by later—

ESTHER. Jeanie, it's my opinion you've treated Sonny pretty shabbily all evening—

JEANIE. Says who?

BETSY. *(Stepping in—in a deep voice)* Says me!

SONNY. I guess I got friends.

HELEN. Now, kids, let's quiet down a little and talk this over—

SONNY. Let 'em fight over me. I like it.

(Crosses to turn on radio. In a moment music fills the

room—not so loud that the dialog cannot be heard above it.)

HELEN. I have a feeling *(Looks up)* we're disturbing James.

LESLIE. He needs it.

HELEN. *(Whirling)* Leslie! What are you doing here?

LESLIE. Sonny invited me.

SONNY. She's all set, Mr. Gardner. Just give her the word.

LESLIE. Is it true, Helen? Will you go out with me this evening?

HELEN. This evening? But you know that's impossible—

SONNY. Remember, Miss Russell—remember what I told you—

TUBBY. *(To PAMELA)* Dance?

PAMELA. Thanks.

(PAMELA and TUBBY dance. ESTHER, JEANIE and BETSY step toward SONNY all at same time. SONNY beams, looking from one to the other, while LESLIE and HELEN continue conversation upstage.)

SONNY. Nobody ever told me the sticks would be like this.

JEANIE. The "sticks"?

SONNY. *(Reaches for her; she turns abruptly away)* Esther?

ESTHER. I don't like what you just said. This isn't the sticks! *(She also turns away.)*

SONNY. *(Turning to BETSY)* Say— Betsy?

BETSY. I was in New York once. It didn't look so hot to me.

(She also turns away. Now all THREE GIRLS have their backs to him.)

SONNY. *(Flabbergasted)* Holy cats and codfish! *(Throws himself, pouting, to sofa.)*

HELEN. *(In her conversation with* LESLIE*)* But I think it would be such a rotten trick, that's all.

*(*JAMES, *dressed for the party, comes down stairs and stands in hall, overhearing the next line.)*

LESLIE. Rotten trick? Do him good. Let the old oaf look after his own relatives. He doesn't hire you for that.

JAMES. Everyone having a good time? *(Steps down to* LESLIE*)* Hard at work, are you, Leslie?

LESLIE. Sure. Want to take it to court?

JAMES. Why don't you forget it, Leslie? Hasn't Helen made it pretty obvious where she stands? *(Turns to* KIDS*)* Hello, hello! Everyone having a time? Good! *(Sees* SONNY*)* Sonny—why don't you dance with one of these pretty young ladies?

SONNY. I'll live without it.

HELEN. *(Stepping up behind* JAMES*)* Leslie has asked me to go out with him, James.

JAMES. *(Turning)* Leslie will try anything. I hope you told him what you think of him.

HELEN. You're pretty sure of yourself, aren't you? And Sonny was right—you didn't say a word about my gown!

JAMES. I beg your pardon?

HELEN. What makes you so sure I won't?

SONNY. Get wise, Miss Russell. Now you're waking up.

JAMES. *(To* HELEN*)* Because you wouldn't do a thing like that at a time like this. You don't care a rap for Leslie Gardner and you know it.

LESLIE. Please don't talk about me as though I weren't here.

JAMES. As far as I'm concerned, you're not.

HELEN. *(Angry)* Well, it just so happens I said I would go—and I'm going!

JAMES. What?

HELEN. Goodbye. *(Takes* LESLIE'S *arm and starts for up Right.)*

JAMES. *(His attitude changing)* Helen—wait! Now wait a minute! You can't. Why, this evening—with all these kids—

BETSY. "Kids"?

JEANIE. How do you like that—"kids"?

ESTHER. Mr. Clark—we're not *children.*

JAMES. *(Whose head has been turning from one to the other)* Now please don't let's get involved—

HELEN. Goodbye, James. *(Starts out French doors.)*

JAMES. Hey— *(Then in an imperative tone)* Helen —I forbid it!

HELEN. Forbid? Isn't he a scream, Leslie? Ready?

LESLIE. He's a scream. *(Flatly)* Ha-ha.

(HELEN *and* LESLIE *exit, with* JAMES *staring after them, angry and helpless.)*

SONNY. She's getting wise.

JAMES. What did you have to do with this?

SONNY. Me? Nothing.

JAMES. Who asked Leslie Gardner here anyway?

SONNY. I did. After he got that list of names for me, I had to do something in return.

JAMES. You mean you made a deal with him?

SONNY. That'd be telling.

JAMES. Sonny—have you ever had an old-fashioned spanking?

SONNY. *(Rising)* What?

JAMES. Because that's what I've half a notion to give you right now. *(Steps toward* SONNY, *who retreats.)*

JEANIE. Goodie!

BETSY. Hurray!

ESTHER. He deserves it.

JAMES. I could probably get some help, too.

SONNY. Now Unc—think of your dignity. And mine.

(He is backing up, JAMES *after him, slowly, step by step.* TUBBY *and* PAMELA *stop dancing.* FREDER-ICKA COLLINS, *a middle-aged lady with a nervous*

nature and a flash camera, appears in French doors, takes all this in.)

JAMES. Maybe that's been my trouble. I've thought of my dignity too much—and not enough about my life!

SONNY. You'll be sorry, Unc.

(JAMES *makes a grab for* SONNY *and* SONNY *breaks away and runs Right. Just at that moment* FREDERICKA, *who has taken in scene, flashes camera.* JAMES *freezes.)*

SONNY. *(To* PAMELA, *as he crosses)* Has he gone off his rocker or something?

JAMES. *(To* FREDERICKA*)* Who are you?

FREDERICKA. Mr. Morgan sent me over to get some pictures for the society page. My name's Fredericka Collins.

JAMES. You wouldn't put a picture like that on your society page?

FREDERICKA. No. I keep those for my private files. Then when I'm unhappy, I can get a lot of laughs. And they're fun at parties.

JAMES. *(Straightening his jacket, back on his dignity)* Why did Morgan send you here?

FREDERICKA. He said someone said there wasn't any freedom of the press in this town—and he wants to prove there is. So I'm supposed to take some informal shots of the party—if you don't mind.

JAMES. I'm not sure. I—

(Before he can complete his sentence, BILL HENLY, *wearing evening clothes, enters through front door.* TUBBY *still has his arm around* PAMELA.)*

PAMELA. Bill!

BILL. *(Standing on step)* I see you're taking care of her, Tubby. *My pal!*

TUBBY. Sure I am!

BILL. You don't have to keep your arm around her to prove it.

JAMES. What's all this?

TUBBY. I'm mighty pleased to keep my arm around her—pal.

BILL. Well, you can drop it now—pal.

PAMELA. *(Replacing* TUBBY'S *hand around her)* Maybe I like it, Mr. Henly.

BILL. Well, *I* don't! I went to a lot of trouble to get over here this evening and at least I don't have to stand around and watch anyone hugging my girl.

PAMELA. I like that! *Your* girl! And where is Harriet?

BILL. I ditched her—for half an hour. I have to go back.

*(*HARRIET *enters through French doors, pushing by* FREDERICKA, *almost knocking her down.)*

HARRIET. I heard that! You did *not* ditch me, Mr. William Henly! I followed you!

TUBBY. You're in a mighty funny spot, Bill. Engaged to one girl—

FREDERICKA. *(The newshound)* Who's engaged?

TUBBY. *(Pointing to* BILL) He is.

BILL. *(Stepping toward* PAMELA) So that's the kind of a girl you are, Pam. I didn't think so—

PAMELA. And what are you doing—out dancing with *her? (Points to* HARRIET.)

BILL. That doesn't count.

JAMES. I suggest we all sit down now and talk quietly—before someone gets hurt here. I suggest—

FREDERICKA. *(Taking over, pushes* TUBBY *aside)* Stand back—let me get a picture of the engaged couple.

BILL. *(Whirling on her)* No, you don't—

HARRIET. Engaged?! Engaged! So that's what you were doing last night!

PAMELA. *(Sweetly, as she takes* BILL'S *arm)* You're masterful, aren't you?

(She smiles into camera as she sees FREDERICKA *raise it.* BILL'S *eyes pop and his hand goes up as though to prevent photo, but he is too late. Flash! The picture is taken.)*

FREDERICKA. Now let me have some names.
JAMES. No! You see, there must be some horrible mistake—
FREDERICKA. *(Taking over, pushes* TUBBY *aside)* Stand back—let me get a picture of the engaged couple. *(Points to* PAMELA.*)*
JEANIE. Pamela Young.

(FREDERICKA *writes this down.)*

PAMELA. His is Bill Henly. Isn't it—darling?
BILL. No! Say, what is this? You can't—
HARRIET. Wait till my father hears about this! Engaged? In one night!
SONNY. *(Crossing to* PAMELA*)* Pam—let me be the first to congratulate you.
JAMES. But—but—but—
BILL. Harriet!
SONNY. Go on home and tell Papa, Harriet. I'd like to see the old pirate's face myself.
HARRIET. *(Stepping to* SONNY*)* What did you call him?
SONNY. I called him an old pirate. That's what everyone around here calls him, isn't it?
JAMES. No. Sonny—don't say that. You'll ruin—
SONNY. But Unc—you called him an old pirate yourself.
HARRIET. *(Whirling)* You did?
JAMES. I?
HARRIET. Papa will be very interested in that. You can't win an election by getting your niece engaged and calling names, you know. It's not ethical.
JAMES. I didn't.
HARRIET. Goodbye, Bill. *(Extends her hand)* I know you're just the victim of circumstances. I hope they

choke you. *(Turns and goes to hall, pauses, turns)* This is probably just what my father needed. *(Near tears)* To win the election— *(Bravely)* What does it matter that *my* heart is smashed?!

BILL. *(Calling after her)* Harriet! Harriet—you don't understand— *(Turns to* PAMELA*)* I hope you're satisfied. I hope—

PAMELA. You don't really have to marry me, Bill. I just got so mad when you started ordering poor Tubby around—after he'd been so sweet.

BILL. Well, you can have him! *(Turns and follows* HARRIET *out, slamming door.)*

TUBBY. I'd be mighty pleased, Pamela—

PAMELA. *(Changing again—to* TUBBY*)* Oh, you shut up! Why does everyone try to get me all mixed up all the time?

JAMES. *(To* FREDERICKA*)* You can't print that picture—it's not the truth.

FREDERICKA. Maybe it isn't true, but it's news, Mister.

TONY. *(The front door opens and* TONY, *the expressman, appears, all dressed up and shining. He smiles broadly)* Which one is Pamela Young?

SONNY. *(Groaning)* Oh!

PAMELA. Who are you?

TONY. I'm Tony. *(Points to* SONNY*)* He told me to come back for the party.

JAMES. *(Whirling on* SONNY*)* You, again!

TONY. Which one is Pamela Young?

(At this point there is the sound of HORNS, and girls' VOICES—many of them—off. ALL *stand for a moment, startled. The horns get closer, louder.)*

JAMES. What's that?

SONNY. *(Leaping up)* It's all right. I know all about it.

JAMES. Sonny—*what is that racket?*

SONNY. *(Beaming)* They came! I wasn't sure they could. *(Starts for French doors)* It's all the girls from

Camp Tuckahoe—for the party. Wasn't it nice they could come? All hundred and twelve of them.

(Goes out, followed by JEANIE, BETSY, ESTHER, *exclaiming ad lib. During the following the NOISE continues outside—many girls' VOICES.)*

JAMES. A hundred and twelve girls—

(FREDERICKA *rushes out to get more pictures.)*

TONY. Will someone please — kindly —please tell me— Where is Pamela Young?

PAMELA. I'm Pamela Young and I'm going upstairs to drink a little arsenic. Goodnight. *(She goes into hall and up stairs.)*

TONY. Arsenic? I don't think I'd like it. *(Then it dawns on him)* But that boy said Miss Young was *my* age!

JAMES. Get out of here! *(To* TUBBY *and* TONY*)* Go on, both of you. Get out. I can't stand any more.

TONY. I'm going, I'm going—only don't be impolite about it. *(Turns and exits through front door.)*
                                        (WARN Curtain.)

TUBBY. *(As* JAMES *sinks to up Left chair, head in hands)* I'm sorry, Mr. Clark. It's sure mighty unpleasant for you. Like my father. He always says he'd rather have an operation than for me to have a party. *(Crosses sadly to French doors.)*

JAMES. What does your father know? I haven't got a home anymore. I haven't got a secretary. I haven't got a girl friend. And I've lost the election. The only thing I *have* got is a housekeeper—

TUBBY. *(As he goes)* I'll never do anyone a favor again.

(CARRIE *enters from living room. She is dressed for traveling and carries a suitcase. She goes directly to* JAMES. *Slowly his head comes up; his eyes meet hers.)*

CARRIE. Mr. Clark—I'm leaving.

JAMES. Carrie—

CARRIE. I can't live in a kitchen that's run by a dog.

JAMES. *(His head up, pleading)* Carrie—listen to me —Carrie—you can't. You—why, you've been like a mother to me.

CARRIE. I don't mind being a mother to *you*, Mr. Clark. Even if you are hard to get along with sometimes. But I won't be related to those two kids! *(Crosses to hall.)*

JAMES. *(Rising—determination in his voice)* Carrie —things are going to change around here!

CARRIE. Good.

JAMES. Carrie—there's going to be a revolution around here! Starting tonight!

CARRIE. Write me a letter. *(Goes out.)*

JAMES. I don't mind a little fun, but this is going too far! *(Starts for French doors)* Sonny! Sonny! Sonny —come in here!

SONNY. *(Off)* Busy, Unc.

JAMES. Very well, then. I'll come and get you!

(He is taking off his jacket and starting out the French doors, murder in his eyes as—

THE CURTAIN FALLS

ACT TWO

SCENE II

SCENE: *The same.*

TIME: *The following Saturday, just after noon.*

AT RISE: *The posters have been removed, and the room is in perfect order. From outside comes the sound of much HAMMERING. Otherwise, it is a quiet, peaceful day, with much sunshine.*

PAMELA, *dressed in casual clothes, is walking*

up and down the room, nervously, thoughtfully.
SONNY, *in a costume a bit more subdued than
usual, sits at desk, working with a screwdriver over
some very small, delicate parts of machinery.*

SONNY. Do you know that for almost one solid week
you've been pacing like that?

PAMELA. I know.

SONNY. You must be tired.—And every time the telephone rings, you break my arm when I reach for it.

PAMELA. I know.

SONNY. Why don't you telephone New York and ask
Jeffrey to come out here?

PAMELA. Jeffrey? I don't want to see Jeffrey.

SONNY. *(Shaking head)* And all because of a simple
little picture in a newspaper.

PAMELA. "Simple little picture?" Do you realize what
Bill's father said to Uncle Jimmie about that picture?
He accused him of trying to marry me off to get rid
of me.

SONNY. Not a bad idea.

PAMELA. And Bill hasn't been near the place since.
I haven't even *seen* him.

SONNY. Your own fiance? Tsk.

PAMELA. And that's not even the worst part. Bill's
President of the Junior Club and it'll be his job to
present the Queen to the Ball this evening. And you
know who that means.

SONNY. Sure. It means Miss Russell.

PAMELA. It means Harriet Morgan! *(Near* SONNY
at desk) Sonny—you don't really think we've got a
chance, do you? With that float out there—and everything that's happened? Besides, Miss Russell's too old
to be Queen.

SONNY. Pam—you're just burned with jealousy, because you want to ride that float.

PAMELA. I do not! *(Crosses to fling herself to sofa)*
And make a fool of myself? After everything that's
happened—and after everything Mr. Morgan's printed
in his paper about Uncle Jimmie—why, people are

liable to boo at the float when it goes by the judging stand today.

SONNY. The old pirate's sure made political capital out of that innocent little remark about his being a pirate, hasn't he? And I'd like to know what's more unethical—that's what he calls it—than what *he's* been doing.

(JAMES *enters from outside through French doors. He is dressed in a conservative suit and seems self-contained, poised, pleasant in manner. He crosses to Center, speaking.*)

JAMES. Well, Sonny—I think the girls are to be congratulated. They've done a fine job on the float. And so have you. Now do you—

SONNY. *(Interrupting)* Unc, I have an idea—

JAMES. *(Sternly but pleasantly)* Sonny, I'm speaking.

SONNY. *(Subsides)* Sorry.

JAMES. Now what I started to say was—do you two have your instructions clear? *(Looks at watch)* The parade begins in exactly one-half an hour. *(His head snaps up as he understands, this late, what* SONNY *has just said)* What did you say just now, Sonny?

SONNY. I said I had an idea. If you—

JAMES. Sonny—I thought I made it pretty clear that you are *not* to *have ideas.* Never again this summer. Never so long as you are under my roof— Now is that understood?

SONNY. Yes, sir.

JAMES. *(In a kinder tone, crossing to* SONNY, *placing arm around him)* I don't mean to be unkind, Sonny. I've adjusted myself to the fact that I have about one chance in twenty of winning the election now. And I'll never be District Attorney. *(Draws away)* But at least I'm master in my own house—and I like it! So, no ideas.

SONNY. Yes, sir.

JAMES. *(Crosses to Left; turns)* But we'll give them a fight, won't we?

SONNY. Yes, sir.

JAMES. Now here's what you're to do. Pam, you'll be driving. Keep the clutch in and try not to use the brake, but go slowly. Sonny, you'll be wearing the clown's uniform—by the way, where is the clown's costume?

PAMELA. It hasn't arrived. And neither has Miss Russell's lion-tamer's costume. And neither has Miss Russell.

JAMES. *(Immediately back to his old self—upset, pacing)* They haven't, eh? And where do you suppose—you don't think—but of course— *(Gets hold of himself—composed again)* Well, don't worry about them. They'll be here.

JEANIE. *(Enters through French doors. In a rush)* Mr. Clark—

JAMES. Yes, Jeanie?

JEANIE. I'm worried about the float, Mr. Clark. Esther and Betsy are quarreling—and when they get mad, it's awful.

JAMES. Don't worry, Jeanie. Have no fear. *(Crosses to sit beside PAMELA on sofa.)*

JEANIE. Yes, sir. *(Crosses to SONNY)* Do you know what they're fighting about?

SONNY. No.

JEANIE. Esther says you have a date with her for the ball tonight. Betsy says you asked her.

SONNY. *(Innocently)* They do?

JEANIE. Yes! What I want to know is—what happened to the date you and I were supposed to have?

SONNY. *(Working hard over machinery)* I'm going with you, Jeanie. You know that.

JEANIE. *(Head high, as she crosses to front door in hall)* That's what I thought. Wait till I tell them! *(Goes out, slamming door.)*

JAMES. *(To PAMELA)* Pamela—I'm worried about you. You've done nothing but mope for a week. I know love is unpleasant—but it shouldn't give you indigestion.

PAMELA. It's just everything, Uncle Jimmie. Just everything!

(In the kitchen the DOG howls mournfully.)

JAMES. It wouldn't be so bad if that dog wasn't so sympathetic. *(DOG howls louder)* But all that noise—

(There is a KNOCK at front door. JAMES turns head.)

JAMES. *(Not quite a command)* Sonny.

SONNY. *(Rising and going to door)* Yes, sir.

JAMES. I think Sonny misses Carrie more than anyone else.

PAMELA. No, he doesn't. I do. I'm not used to cooking three meals a day.

JAMES. Good for you.—Discipline.

(SONNY has opened door. TONY stands there. He has still another box.)

SONNY. *(Returning to desk)* Come on in, Tony.

TONY. Okay! *(Enters and places box at Center; he looks around)* Things aint what they used to be around here, I'd say. Who signs? *(Holds up delivery book.)*

JAMES. *(Crossing and taking book)* I'll take it.

PAMELA. *(Rising and crossing to box)* It's the costumes! *(Starts opening box)* Help me, Tony.

TONY. Sure! I'm an obliging fellow. Hold no grudges. *(He is opening box with PAMELA)* Invited to a party—kicked out of a party. Still—no grudges.

SONNY. *(Hard at work again at desk)* I'm sorry about that, Tony.

TONY. Don't matter. You know what I did that night? Went out and made up with my girl. Looked so spruce she just fell in love all over again. *(Takes out costumes: a circus clown's, a feminine trapeze artist's or lion-tamer's and a lion or bear costume. Holds them up)* Love is about the greatest thing in the world, ain't it?

(Hearing this, PAMELA *bursts into a wail and goes to sofa, throws herself onto it, crying.* TONY *looks at her, puzzled. In the kitchen the DOG howls again.* TONY *stares, puzzled. Through the following, whenever* PAMELA *cries, the dog yowls in unison with her.* NOTE ON COSTUMES: *The clown's and lion-tamer's costumes are easily obtained at any good costumer's. Many homes have clown's costumes for Hallowe'en use. And the lion-tamer's can be easily made, with or without the help of the school's Home Economics classes. As to the lion's costume—this also can be obtained at a costumer's, but it is not necessary to the play and can be eliminated simply by cutting out the action and business associated with it on the following pages. However, with a little ingenuity, a "bear rug" can be converted easily and simply into a bear costume. In the event any or all of these costumes are difficult to obtain for your production, they need never be worn; and in this case any pieces of cloth can be used and carried by the various actors in the next two scenes.)*

TONY. *(To* PAMELA*)* Don't let the costume scare you, kid. *(Holds up lion or bear)* Just a skin. Dead. Can't bite. *(He places it over his head)* See?

JAMES. It's not that, Tony. It's what you said about love.

*(*PAMELA *cries louder.)*

TONY. *(Bewildered)* Love?

*(*PAMELA *kicks her feet and cries louder. The DOG sets up a tremendous racket.)*

JAMES. I don't think we'd better mention that word again.

TONY. *(Puzzled, as he picks up a snake-whip from bottom of costume box)* Okay! *(Holds up whip)* Whip and everything. *(He cracks the whip once—loud.)*

HELEN. *(Wearing a summer sleeveless dress, enters through French doors. She is quiet and in pain. Her face and arms are brilliant red—sunburn)* James—

JAMES. *(Stares at her, his eyes widen)* Helen!

HELEN. Hello! I've been playing golf.

JAMES. So I see. *(Picks up lion-tamer's costume and tosses it at her)* Do you realize we have only about fifteen minutes before we start?

SONNY. *(Working even more desperately, quietly, bending low)* Fifteen minutes Oh, my gosh!

HELEN. I'll change right away. *(Crosses to hall and starts up stairs)* But I had a lovely time—*with Leslie.* *(Goes off.)*

JAMES. *(Crossing to stairs and shouting up)* Good! *(He realizes this is weak and turns to room.* TONY *is staring at him)* Well—what do *you* want?

TONY. My book, please.

JAMES. Oh! *(Shoves delivery book at* TONY*)* How'd you like to be in a parade?

TONY. Fine! I got the afternoon off anyway.

JAMES. All you have to do is crack the whip.

TONY. That's easy.

JAMES. And don't hit anybody.

TONY. That's harder.

JAMES. Now go outside and practice.

TONY. You crack a mean whip yourself, don't you? *(Goes out front door, taking whip.)*

JAMES. *(Crossing to* SONNY*)* Sonny—what are you doing?

SONNY. Fixing something.

(PAMELA *lifts her head; looks at them.)*

JAMES. *(Suspicious—with threatening quietness)* Sonny—what—are—you—*fixing—?*

SONNY. I'll get it. Just leave me alone now, Unc— I'll get it together.

JAMES. *(His wrath rising)* Sonny—what is that—that mess you have there?

SONNY. *(Looking up at him—shrugging)* You really want to know

PAMELA. Sonny!

JAMES. I most certainly *do* want to know!!

SONNY. Okay, then— It's the starter in the car.

JAMES. The starter? The—??

SONNY. Nov.' control yourself, Unc. Get hold of yourself.

JAMES. Does that mean my car won't start again?

SONNY. Not if you don't stop badgering me and let me fix it.

JAMES. Great jumping Jehosevet!

(The hammering — which has been lessening and mingling with the sound of the WHIP CRACK-ING outside—now comes to a full stop.)

PAMELA. Sonny— *(Rises)* Sonny—without the car—

JAMES. *(Taking a deep breath)* Without the car—we can't pull the float!

HELEN. *(At this inopportune moment* HELEN *appears in hall, wearing the lion-tamer's costume, which is very short. Her face and arms are brilliant red, and below her knees her legs are the same color; above her knees, however, they are not red at all. She presents a ludicrous, sad picture and knows it)* James—I think there's something we ought to discuss—

*(*JAMES *turns and sees her. He gasps. So does* PAMELA.*)*

JAMES. Helen! *Helen!*

HELEN. I always sunburn so easily. I should have remembered, shouldn't I?

JAMES. *(Beginning to laugh)* Ha-ha-ha. Ha-ha. *(Sinks to up Left chair, laughing)* Good Lord—what a mess! Helen—what a— *(He is laughing.)*

SONNY. *(Crossing to him)* Unc—

PAMELA. Uncle Jimmie—

HELEN. I don't think it's *that* funny.

SONNY. It's the heat. It's—it's everything put together.

PAMELA. Maybe we better call a doctor.

(JEANIE *bursts through the front door, followed by* BETSY *and* ESTHER. *Crepe paper streams from all of them, and they are tousled and torn.*)

JEANIE. (*To* SONNY) Now see what you've done!

SONNY. What—?

JEANIE. They started fighting!

ESTHER. *We* started fighting?

BETSY. *You* started it, Jeanie.

JEANIE. I simply said you were taking me to the ball.

BETSY. Which is a blank-faced lie!

JEANIE. But you ought to see the float! They tore up the float! It looks terrible!

(JAMES *bursts into more laughter.* ALL *turn to him.*)

JEANIE. What's the matter with him?

HELEN. We've only got ten minutes.

SONNY. Pam—Pam—you're going to be Queen!

PAMELA. What?

SONNY. (*To* HELEN) Take her upstairs and get her into that costume.

HELEN. That's the only sensible thing I've heard all day.

PAMELA. (*Amazed and pleased*) I'm going to be Queen!

HELEN. (*Rushing to stairs*) Hurry up.

PAMELA. (*As she dashes after* HELEN) I'll show Mr. William Henly!

JEANIE. But Sonny—the car won't go—

SONNY. Jeanie—you get on that telephone. Get those girls down here. *All* of them! (JAMES *laughs once again*) You get hold of yourself or I'll call a doctor.

JAMES. *(Rising—with broad gestures)* But I'm relaxing. Remember? I'm having a good time. I never had a good time before. Well, from now on— *(Laughs again.)*

JEANIE. *(At telephone now)* What'll I say?

SONNY. Tell them we want all hundred and twelve of them. They're going to pull a float!

JEANIE. *(Picking up phone)* I think you're crazy, too. *(Into telephone)* Get me 17534, Operator.

JAMES. *(Picking up clown's costume)* And do you know what I'm going to do?

SONNY. *(Rushing to front door, calling)* Tony! Tony!

JAMES. *(Beginning to tear off coat and climbing into clown's costume)* I'm going to be in that parade myself! I always wanted to be a clown!

(TONY *enters at front door.)*

SONNY. Tony—you're going to ride on the front of the float and crack that whip over the heads of one hundred and twelve girls. Think you can do it?

TONY. Do it? *(Smiling broadly)* I'll love it. And if you want to go faster, just let me know! *(Exits, cracking whip.)*

JAMES. We're going to make history!

SONNY. *(Climbing into lion's costume)* Grrrrr! *(Pulls it over his head and gets down on all fours.)*

JEANIE. They're all nuts. *(Into telephone)* Hello! Hello!

(HELEN *comes down, wearing her dress. She looks around room. Her eyes open and open again.)*

JEANIE. *(Into telephone)* This is Jeanie! Send the girls! Send all of them! We've got a job to do—and then we're all going to a dance! *(WARN Curtain.)*

SONNY. *(Crossing to stairs and calling up, with a growl)* Pam—Pam! Hurry up!

(PAMELA *comes down, looking resplendent in the costume.*)

HELEN. *(To* JAMES*)* What's come over you?

JAMES. Me? Nothing! I'm having fun—for the first
time in my life! Sonny—lead the way.

HELEN. James—your dignity.

JAMES. Let my dignity look out for itself! *(He
bounds out the French doors, followed by* BETSY *and*
ESTHER.*)*

BETSY. *(As she goes)* Isn't he cute?

HELEN. *(Following)* He's cute all right.

(SONNY *and* PAMELA *face each other on step.*)

SONNY. Pamela—isn't it wonderful?

PAMELA. Do I look all right, Sonny? *(Goes out front
door.)*

SONNY. At a time like this that's all a gal can think
of!

CARRIE. *(Carrying her traveling bag and dressed for
traveling as in last scene, enters from living room)* Mr.
Clark—I've come back. Mr. Clark—

(She sees SONNY, *who has pulled the lion's face over
his head. She stands frozen.* SONNY, *seeing her,
drops to all fours and with a ferocious growl
starts in her direction.* CARRIE *drops her bag,
screams and turns.* SONNY *lopes after her on all
fours, growling loudly.)*

FAST CURTAIN

ACT THREE

SCENE: *The same.*

TIME: *Several hours later.*

AT RISE: *The room is empty. Silence. After a long pause the front door opens and* HELEN *enters. Her face is very long; her attitude is weary, resigned, sad. She walks—at a funeral pace—to the Right end of the sofa and sits. She stares straight ahead and then her head sinks down. She stares solemnly at the floor for a moment.*

Then the door opens again and this time PAMELA *—walking equally slowly and looking unhappy, without a word or gesture—crosses to desk. She wears her lion tamer's costume. She sits behind it, her chin in her hands, staring ahead. A long moment.*

Then the front door opens again and this time SONNY *appears. He wears the lion's costume, the face thrown back, and he looks equally despondent. He trudges with very slow feet to the Up Left chair and sinks slowly into it.*

The silence continues. After a suitable length of time, BETSY *enters through the French doors. She crosses Center, looks from* HELEN *to* SONNY *to* PAMELA.

BETSY. I thought it was fun.

(HELEN, PAMELA *and* SONNY *turn to her as with one motion, their heads moving slowly.)*

HELEN. That's nice.

77

BETSY. Oh, I know it didn't do Mr. Clark any good, but people certainly laughed.

SONNY. *(Bitterly)* Ha-ha!

(ESTHER *enters through front door; stands on step.* SONNY, HELEN *and* PAMELA *face front again—blankly.*)

ESTHER. Wasn't it awful? *(No answer)* Even *I* was mortified.

PAMELA. *(Very softly)* Shut up.

ESTHER. What did I say?

BETSY. *(As she crosses to up Right chair)* I went to a wake once. It was just like this.

SONNY. I'm the corpse.

HELEN. James is the corpse.

PAMELA. Why talk?

(ESTHER *crosses to sit on hassock in front of radio at Right. There is another pause. During this pause a sound is heard off Left: a dog's low and mournful WAIL.*)

ESTHER. What's that?

SONNY. A banshee in the kitchen.

PAM. Shut up.

BETSY. Well, I don't care. With that whip cracking— *(She looks at* SONNY*)* and you prancing around like a stage-struck lion and Mr. Clark in that clown costume —I almost died laughing.

PAM. Too bad you didn't make it.

ESTHER. *(To* SONNY*)* I didn't know your uncle was that athletic.

HELEN. Those were his reducing exercises.

BETSY. He could get a job in a circus.

HELEN. He may need to.

PAMELA. It was all your fault, Sonny.

SONNY. *(With his first show of spirit)* My fault?

PAMELA. If you hadn't—

HELEN. I think we can do without that, Kids. Remember, this is a funeral.

PAMELA. Sorry.

SONNY. You're probably right.

(At this point the front door opens again and TONY, *carrying his whip, enters.)*

TONY. *(On step)* Any animals you want trained around here?

(The dog WAILS in the kitchen.)

HELEN. What I don't understand is—who is that man?

TONY. *(As he steps toward her. Cheerfully)* I'm Tony.

HELEN. How'd you get in on this?

TONY. It wasn't hard.

SONNY. Pam—

PAMELA. Yeah?

SONNY. I think we should have gone to Mexico.

PAMELA. I feel so sorry for him I could cry.

HELEN. I won't even know what to say to him.

SONNY. I feel so bad. Maybe I ought to go to work and fix everything that's broken in the house.

HELEN. *(Ironically)* Sure! Cheer him up.

PAMELA. Maybe he won't even come home. If I were Uncle Jimmie, I'd join the Navy and see the world.

(A WHISTLE is heard off Right, approaching. SONNY, HELEN *and* PAMELA *exchange glances.)*

TONY. Nobody ought to whistle at a time like this.

SONNY. Some people would whistle in a graveyard.

(The WHISTLE comes closer, and JAMES, *with deep red lipstick circles on the end of his nose, the point of his chin and both cheeks, still wearing his*

clown's costume and still looking very cheerful and gay, enters through the French doors.)

JAMES. *(Brightly)* Well, well, well!—My bright and happy family all together again.

HELEN. *(In an awed whisper)* James! ⎫

SONNY. *(Half-rising from his chair)* Unc! ⎬ *(Together)*

PAMELA. *(Her eyes wide)* Uncle Jimmie! ⎭

JAMES. What's everyone so solemn about? Why all the gloom in my happy home?

SONNY. You can drop the act now, Unc. You were great out there, but you can settle down now.

JAMES. "Act"? "Settle down"? Don't know what you're talking about. *(Crosses around Left end of sofa to look past TONY toward HELEN)* —So you've joined the mourners, too, have you, Helen? *(Shakes head)* And here I thought I was pretty good.

BETSY. *(Rising)* Oh, you were, Mr. Clark! I died laughing myself.

JAMES. *(With a little bow toward BETSY)* Thank you. *(Then to HELEN—with a gesture)* You see—my public.

HELEN. I see. Your *dead* public.

JAMES. *(Turning to SONNY and PAMELA)* And Sonny! And Pam! Of all people! Why, Pam, I thought nothing but boy friends could ever get your chin down. And Sonny—except for the night you and I had our battle—I've never seen you look so low— *(Crosses to Center)* What could the matter be?

TONY. *(In a little voice)* I know.

JAMES. *(Whirling)* You do? What is it, Mr.—Mr.— I'm sorry, I didn't get your name.

TONY. Tony. Everyone calls me Tony. Except my girl. She calls me Monkeyface.

JAMES. I'll tell you what, Tony—just to show how much I like you, *I'll* call you Monkeyface too.

TONY. Thanks, Mr. Clark.

JAMES. Not at all. And just to show how much you

like me, I want you to call me what my girl calls me.

TONY. Sure. What's that?

JAMES. *(With a glance toward* HELEN*)* Fuss-budget.

HELEN. *(Rising)* James—you're making me angry. I know you want to take this in the best of spirits and show you're a good sport. Well, you've shown it. We all admire you. *(To* OTHERS*)* Don't we? (SONNY *claps his hands twice, softly)* There. But enough is enough!

JAMES. *(Turning to* SONNY*)* What about a little music, Sonny? Where's that awful saxophone of yours?

SONNY. *(Rising and crossing behind sofa to address* HELEN*)* Miss Russell—I think we'd better go a little slow. Humor him, maybe. I saw it happen in here earlier this afternoon. I think it's kind of like shock. *(Makes circles in air around his ears and gestures to* JAMES*)* He's stunned. He'll come out of it.

JAMES. I resent that! Everyone from Helen to that dog out there has been telling me to take things more lightly, to take it easy, to relax. Well, I'm letting myself go! *(Crosses to* PAMELA*)* I feel years younger. I almost feel as young as Pam. Pretty soon I'm going to ask her to tell me how to get my girl back.

PAMELA. *(Mournfully)* Uncle Jimmie—your whole career is ruined. Don't you *care?*

JAMES. Care? Of course I don't care. What's a career? You didn't care. Sonny didn't care. Why should *I* care?

PAMELA. You're just trying to make us feel worse.

TONY. I think you're right, Mr.—Fuss-budget.

JAMES. *(With a bow toward him)* Thank you, Monkeyface.

TONY. *(Waving his hand)* Any time.

JAMES. *(Heartily, as he crosses to* TONY*)* You know —I'm glad you stopped by. You add a note of gaiety to the afternoon.

TONY. Fuss-budget—let me tell you: you were a riot out there today!

JAMES. I didn't know I had it in me. Why, man—I could be a riot *any* time!

(There is a KNOCK at front door. JAMES crosses to answer.)

SONNY. By the way—where's Jeanie?
BETSY. What do *you* care?
ESTHER. *(To* SONNY*)* So what?

(JAMES opens door. It is FREDERICKA COLLINS, the news-photographer.)

FREDERICKA. How do you do? I know you don't want to see me around here, but—
JAMES. *(Throwing open the door and gesturing her into room)* "Don't want to see you"? Where did you ever get that idea? Why, you're the lady who tried to marry my niece off to that nice young Bill Henly. Only I'm sorry to say it didn't work.

(Off Left the dog HOWLS once—mournfully.)

FREDERICKA. *(Studying* JAMES*)* It didn't work, eh?
JAMES. No. Too bad, too. Bill Henly hasn't been seen since.
FREDERICKA. I know the type. *(To* PAMELA*)* I'm sorry, Miss. *(Again the dog HOWLS sadly in the kitchen)* What's that?
JAMES. Oh, him. That's just a dog. He's sensitive. When Pamela feels bad, he cries for her. But don't mind him. We don't want him chasing you away. He chased my housekeeper away. Nice lady. Used to cook all my meals. Doesn't seem like home since she went away.
FREDERICKA. *(Still studying* JAMES*)* Too bad.
JAMES. Yes, isn't it? But one must take it easy. One must relax, you know. Can't let things bother one, can one?
FREDERICKA. *(Turning to room)* How'd they ever manage to get this nut into a nut's costume?
JAMES. *(Mockingly)* Miss Collins, I'm insulted. You have wounded me deeply.

SONNY. *(Sliding to a position behind* FREDERICKA*)*
Be a nice gal, Miss. Play along.

HELEN. Sonny—will you stop that? !

FREDERICKA. "Play along"? Say, do you mean—

(She stares at JAMES, *who smiles benignly.)*

SONNY. Shock—

HELEN. Sonny, don't be childish!

FREDERICKA. Shock, eh? Well, after what I saw here
last week, I'm not surprised. I was shocked myself.
(Business-like now, she taps camera) —Mr. Morgan
sent me over—

JAMES. *(Pleased)* Mister Morgan? Not Henry Morgan? The new President of the Somerset Country Club?
(Turns to OTHERS*)* Did you hear that? Wasn't that
kind of him?

FREDERICKA. He wants me to get some pictures for
the paper.

JAMES. Of the defeated candidate, you mean?

HELEN. You're not defeated yet!

JAMES. Now Helen—we must face facts. The mem-
bers are voting right now—and as Mr. Morgan knows,
they won't vote for me. *(To* FREDERICKA*)* All right,
now—you just tell me what you want? Shall I sit at
the desk and weep?

*(*PAMELA *rises from desk and moves to Left.)*

FREDERICKA. You want to wear that costume?

JAMES. *(As he sits)* This? Of course. I think it's
handsome. I only wish I'd thought of wearing it before.
Looks better than golf-clothes, don't you think? *(He
places feet on desk)* You can *relax* in it better— Why,
do you know, Miss Collins—if I'd worn this a year or
two ago, even a week ago, I might not have lost my
girl.

*(*FREDERICKA *lifts camera at Center, focussing it on*

James. Tony *crosses to Up Center to address*
James.)

Tony. Listen, Fuss-budget.
James. Yes, Monkeyface?

(Fredericka *lowers camera to stare wonderingly at
the two of them.)*

Tony. Don't worry about that losing your girl stuff.
I lost my girl, you know.
James. You *did?*
Tony. Sure. But she came back to me. Right now
she loves me more than ever.
James. That's wonderful. Let me congratulate you.
Fredericka. *(Turning to* Sonny *and* Helen*)* Say
—have I got the right man? I'm supposed to take a
picture of Mr. James Clark, who ran for President in
the Country Club.
Sonny. *(Pointing)* You got him.
Fredericka. But the man I'm supposed to shoot is a
lawyer. Going to run for District Attorney.
Sonny. You got him.
Fredericka. *(Turning to* James; *lifting camera)*
I get the nuttiest assignments.

(Flash! She has taken the picture. James *was smiling
into camera. The front door opens slowly and* Carrie's *head appears.)*

Carrie. Oh, Mr. Clark—? *(*All *turn to door)* Oh,
Mr. Clark—?
James. *(Rising)* Carrie! *(Crosses swiftly to hall)*
Carrie—you've come back.
Carrie. *(Edging in)* Not yet I haven't!
James. Of course you have, Carrie. *(Takes her arm)*
Come on in and meet the folks. Tony—this is Carrie.
The lady I told you about, remember?
Tony. Your girl friend?
James. No, the other one. The one I miss so much.

HELEN. *(Sitting on sofa again)* I like that!

CARRIE. *(Looking at* TONY*)* We've met. *(Turns to* SONNY*)* Think you're smart, don't you, young fellow? Scaring ten years off a lady's life. *(Turns to* JAMES*)* Well, I saw the parade. And I must say you surprised me, Mr. Clark. Why, you're a bigger fool than I thought you were.

JAMES. Thank you, Carrie. That means a lot, coming from you.

CARRIE. I really laughed. Made me forget everything. *(As she crosses to living room door)* I'm going back to work. *(Turns at door)* Mr. Clark, if they don't elect you, the world's going to the dogs. *(On the word "dogs" there is a BARK from the kitchen.* CARRIE *starts)* Dogs! I almost forgot that darned dog! *(As she turns to march into living room)* Well, from now on what's good enough for the rest of us, is good enough for him! (CARRIE *goes out.)*

FREDERICKA. Now I better get one of the lion-tamer, here.

PAMELA. No. You don't want a picture of me. I don't want my face in that paper again.

SONNY. Without Bill, she means.

JAMES. She'd feel lonely.

(TUBBY *and* JEANIE *enter through French doors. They are holding hands as they cross toward Center.)*

SONNY. Jeanie!

JEANIE. *(To* JAMES—*pointedly ignoring* SONNY*)* Mr. Clark—I just want to warn you. Our Counsellor at Camp Tuckahoe—

SONNY. Jeanie—What are you doing with *him?*

TUBBY. *(Smiling—to* SONNY*)* We're going to the ball together. Tonight.

JEANIE. *(To* JAMES*)* Our counsellor, Mr. Clark— She's Irish. And you know the Irish.

TONY. *(Taking a step to Center)* And what's the matter with the Irish?

JEANIE. Are you Irish?

TONY. No.—But my girl is.

JEANIE. But she has an awful temper. And she says those girls pulling the float with that man cracking the whip—she said it was undignified. She gets everything all mixed up, too. She says she's going to drop by—

JAMES. *(Always the gentleman)* We'll be very glad to have her.

JEANIE. That's what I'm trying to say, Mr. Clark. You won't. You know the Irish temper.

TONY. Please don't say a word about the Irish in my presence, Miss.

JEANIE. Who *is* that?

JAMES. But why should this lady be angry?

JEANIE. She says you don't know how to raise your son. *(Glances over her shoulder at* SONNY.)

JAMES. My *son?*

JEANIE. I told you she gets everything mixed up. And she won't let anyone explain to her.

SONNY. Well, *I'll* explain to her. My uncle's got enough trouble. If anyone thought I was his son, he'd *really* have to leave town.

TUBBY. That's what I been telling Jeanie.

SONNY. Oh, you have, have you? *(Crosses in front of* TUBBY *to* JEANIE*)* Listen to me, Jeanie—

JEANIE. *(Facing him)* I've had enough! You've bounced back and forth like a tennis ball and I'm fed up. Take Esther to the ball—

BETSY. Esther? He's taking me!

JEANIE. Or take Betsy—

ESTHER. He can't do that!

JEANIE. Only leave me utterly and entirely alone. A-l-o-n-e. Period. *(Takes* TUBBY's *hand)* Goodbye, all!

(TUBBY *and* JEANIE *exit through front door.*)

SONNY. *(Staring after them)* Women are so darned fickle! *(Turns and flings himself into up Right chair.)*

PAMELA. *(Crossing to place her arm around* SONNY*)* I never thought I'd ever feel sorry for *you.*

(In the kitchen, the dog HOWLS again. FREDERICKA *turns and starts Left.)*

FREDERICKA. I think I better get a picture of that dog. *(Exits into living room.)*

SONNY. Love! Love! If it wasn't for love—

PAMELA. *(Correcting)* Weren't—

SONNY. If it weren't for love—the world'd be a lot better off.

JAMES. Yes, but Sonny—would it go around as fast? That's the.question. Monkeyface, what would you say?

TONY. Love? I can tell you all about it. In the first place, you gotta look at it philosophically, as they say. Like those boxes I deliver, day in and day out. I never know what's in 'em. I just carry 'em around and treat 'em nice. It's the same with women. *(Sits behind desk and* JAMES *sits on desk, raptly listening, nodding)* You never know what's inside.

HELEN. Do you think they'll telephone?

PAMELA. How else would we know?

HELEN. I suppose they will.

JAMES. *(To* TONY*)* I've found love is a difficult matter about which to make up your mind. I waited eight years— *(Looks over his shoulder at* HELEN *and calls out, louder) Eight years*—to find out I was is love. And when I realized it, I was too late. My girl had fallen for an athlete with muscles and no brains.

BETSY. This waiting's killing me.

SONNY. Relax— *(He realizes what he has said and his hand goes quickly over his mouth.)*

HELEN. *(Calling over to* JAMES*)* You can get a lot older in eight years!

JAMES. Not me! I feel younger today than I've felt in twenty years!

PAMELA. Love is silly. I'm not going to look at a man again—any man—until the day I die!

(In the kitchen the dog HOWLS again. Then there is a KNOCK at the front door. ALL *look into hall*

as Mr. Morgan's *head appears around door. He is beaming.)*

Mr. Morgan. May I come in?
James. *(Crossing to hall)* Mr. Morgan? *(To Others)* Isn't this a surprise? Look who's here. It's Mr. Morgan!

(Mr. Morgan *takes one look at* James *and bursts into laughter. The* Others *wait for this to subside.* Harriet *enters behind* Mr. Morgan. *She can wear the costume she wore in parade—as The Goddess of Honesty—or attractive summer dress.)*

Harriet. Daddy!
Mr. Morgan. I'm sorry. *(Wiping his eyes)* I can't help it. Every time I see Mr. James Clark with that stuff on his face— *(He goes off into another great gale of laughter.)*
Harriet. *(Moving into room and glancing around hopefully)* Hello, everybody!
Pamela. *(Looking hopefully behind* Mr. Morgan*)* Hello—

(While Harriet *searches around room,* Pamela *looks out door.)*

James. I hope everyone found me so amusing— Mister Morgan! (James *crosses down Left.)*
Tony. Sure they did, Fuss-budget.
Mr. Morgan. *(Stepping into room and looking around)* Everybody thought you were funny, Mr. Clark— *(Hears what* Tony *has said)* "Fuss-budget"? Say, that's good! *(He starts laughing all over again.)*
Helen. James—are you going to stand there and be insulted by this pirate?
Mr. Morgan. *(The laughter stops abruptly.* Mr. Morgan's *eyes narrow as he crosses to face* Helen*)* Pirate! Now, that's a nasty word I don't like! I don't like it at all! It was credited to my worthy opponent

here and it seems to have caught on. I see people snickering behind my back all over town. And I don't like it!

HELEN. That must be because people have an idea James was right.

MR. MORGAN. *(Whirling to face* JAMES*)* Then you *did* say it? Well, I don't mind saying I consider that a pretty low and insulting way to try to win a Club election—calling your opponent names of that nature.

JAMES. Mr. Morgan—I didn't call you a pirate.

MR. MORGAN. *(Pleased)* You didn't? Then—

JAMES. No, I didn't. Why, if I started calling you names, Mr. Morgan—you don't think I'd stop with pirate, do you?

MR. MORGAN. Now listen here—

JAMES. Just off-hand I can think of a million others. There's hypocrite, for one. And there's mean, stingy, egotistical, dictatorial—

MR. MORGAN. *(Crosses slowly to* JAMES *before he speaks)* That's enough!

HARRIET. *(Up Right, where* PAMELA *has crossed to look out French doors hopefully)* Have you lost something?

PAMELA. *(Sweetly)* No. Have you?

MR. MORGAN. I've done a great many things for this town—

HARRIET. *(To* PAMELA*)* I saw you looking—

PAMELA. You were looking, too.

HARRIET. I was *not* looking.

MR. MORGAN. *(Who has turned to face them, his face red)* I'll wait until you two have finished.

HARRIET. Sorry, Daddy.

PAMELA. I'm not.

MR. MORGAN. *(Turning to* JAMES *again)* I own more property in this town than any other individual—

JAMES. And more mortgages—

MR. MORGAN. Including mortgages. And in all my dealings with everyone, great and small—

HELEN. That's not what most people think.

MR. MORGAN. *(Turning, thin-lipped to* HELEN*)* Will

you kindly let me finish? *(Again to* James*)* I have been the soul of honesty and as kind as a saint. I have—

PAMELA. *(To* HARRIET*)* Isn't he with you?

MR. MORGAN. *(His hand waving as he tries to complete a sentence)* I have lived by the Law and in the eyes of my fellow-citizens—

HARRIET. No. I thought he might be here.

(Slowly MR. MORGAN'S *hand comes down and he turns again, his temper under strained control, to look at* HARRIET *and* PAMELA.*)*

PAMELA. Don't you know where he is?

HARRIET. I haven't seen him for a week.

MR. MORGAN. *(Loud) Harriet! (Then softer)* Harriet—your poor old father is trying to say something.

PAMELA. *(Excited)* Did you hear that? Sonny! Miss Russell! Did you hear? She hasn't seen Bill either!

MR. MORGAN. What's the matter with *her?*

PAMELA. *(Crossing excitedly to* JAMES*)* Uncle Jimmie—did you hear? Isn't that heavenly! He's disappeared. *(She hugs* JAMES, *standing between him and* MR. MORGAN.*)*

JAMES. That's dandy, Pam. Now all we have to do is find him. Between Sonny and yourself, that oughtn't to be hard.

MR. MORGAN. May I ask what this young lady is talking about?

JAMES. Love, Mr. Morgan. You wouldn't know anything about that.

MR. MORGAN. Now you sound just like my wife.

PAMELA. *(Turning on him)* And she's probably right, too!

MR. MORGAN. What? What did you say?

PAMELA. Your wife! She's probably right! You don't know anything about love! You don't love anyone, probably. Even your daughter! She's been upset all week and worried about Bill and you didn't even know it.

MR. MORGAN. Young lady, I detest Bill Henly!

PAMELA. That's what's the matter with you. You detest everybody but yourself! If you had a little kindness and understanding about people, the whole town wouldn't be calling you names right this minute!

HARRIET. *(Stepping toward Center)* Daddy— (MR. MORGAN *turns to her)* She's right.

MR. MORGAN. *(Ready to burst)* What? !

HARRIET. Yes, she is. Mother always says it, and now I believe it.

MR. MORGAN. *(Crossing to* HARRIET*)* You listen to me, young lady—just because you've come to visit a bughouse, don't start acting like a bug!

JAMES. Mr. Morgan, you are speaking of the house I love.

MR. MORGAN. *(Returning to* JAMES*)* And you—I don't understand you at all! Cutting up like a two-year-old out there today. Throwing your career away! Behaving as though you'd lost your mind—

JAMES. No, not lost it, Mr. Morgan. Found it. You see, I used to be a little like you myself. I didn't know what a good time was—not really a good time. I was all wrapped up in my work and myself. Well, I've looked outside myself today—and I've seen a whole new world I didn't even know existed.

MR. MORGAN. Well, you'll need a new world after today. Because I'll make this one so hot you won't want to live in it!

HARRIET. *(Stepping in again)* That's what I mean, Daddy. You're always fighting people and hurting people. And I'm getting to be just like you. And I don't like it! It makes me unhappy. *(She turns away.)*

MR. MORGAN. Harriet— *(Almost tenderly)* Harriet —what is all this? *(He whirls on* JAMES*)* You're the cause of all this.

JAMES. If I am, I'm glad, Mr. Morgan.

MR. MORGAN. Listen to me, you—this town knows what I've done for it. And so does the Country Club!

TONY. Say— (ALL *turn to him)* Are you the Mr. Henry Morgan who runs the bank?

MR. MORGAN. I am, sir.

TONY. Well, don't be so proud of it.

MR. MORGAN. What—?!

TONY. You pushed my brother right out of his house because he couldn't pay two months on his mortgage.

JAMES. I'm afraid that's what the town *really* thinks of you, Mr. Morgan.

TONY. And my brother—he moved right in with me. With seven kids. You ought to see my place now.

MR. MORGAN. *(Bewildered)* What is all this? I just came here to say your act was funny. I—

HELEN. Oh, no, you didn't. You came here to gloat because you were sure you'd won the election.

(There is a pause.)

MR. MORGAN. Well, I'll be darned!

LESLIE. *(Appears at front door and stands in hall. He is smiling)* Hello, all!

(ALL turn. MR. MORGAN, subdued, thoughtful, goes to sit on sofa.)

SONNY. Mr. Gardner—who won?

LESLIE. They're still counting. But I'll make bets around here.

JAMES. Come right in Leslie. Make yourself at home. Think you can find room? *(Goes to him and shakes his hand)* I'm sure glad you dropped by.

LESLIE. *(Surprised)* You are? Well, I just came by to get Helen. She's going to the ball with me.

JAMES. She is? Well, that's nice. I hope you have a good time. Make them play a lot of waltzes. Helen likes waltzes.

HELEN. *(Near tears suddenly)* James! James, how could you?

JAMES. I'm taking it easy. I'm following advice!

LESLIE. You won't feel so gay when you find out Mr. Morgan won the election. *(Sees MR. MORGAN; crosses to him)* —How do you do, Mr. Morgan?

MR. MORGAN. *(Irascibly)* Can't you see I'm thinking?

LESLIE. Don't worry, Mr. Morgan. He hasn't got a chance in a million.

MR. MORGAN. I'm not thinking about that.

LESLIE. *(Crossing to* JAMES*)* Too bad, old boy.

JAMES. I'm as young as you are. Younger.

LESLIE. Ready, Helen? *(Crosses to her, at Right.)*

HELEN. I—I don't know. *(She is looking at* JAMES.*)*

JAMES. You may as well go, Helen. After all, Leslie knows. It's all over but the shouting.

*(*HELEN *turns on her heel—so that* JAMES *can't see her face.)*

SONNY. I'm getting tired of all these condolences.

BETSY. So am I.

ESTHER. Me, too.

(They are standing together.)

TONY. *(He is standing to Right of hall, near wall)* Got enough people here—let's have a party.

(At this point MISS FRANCES SHAUGHNESSY, *the Camp Counsellor, knocks and enters front door.* MISS SHAUGHNESSY *is a huge, athletic, domineering type with a deep, raucous voice.)*

MISS SHAUGHNESSY. Anybody home?

*(*ALL *except* MR. MORGAN *turn.* TONY *freezes against wall.)*

BETSY. Miss Shaughnessy!

ESTHER. Miss Shaughnessy! What are you doing here?

MISS SHAUGHNESSY. *(Marching into room)* Where is he? *(Her eyes light on* MR. MORGAN*)* Are you the one? I just want to tell you that—as Counsellor of

Camp Tuckahoe—I think you have behaved in a criminal and vicious manner—and if I had the authority, I'd sue.

JAMES. I'll take the case.

MISS SHAUGHNESSY. *(Staring at* JAMES*)* And who, may I ask, are you?

JAMES. My name's Clark. I'm a lawyer, and if you need a good one—

MISS SHAUGHNESSY. *(Turning to* MR. MORGAN, *who is staring at her)* I apologize, sir. I thought you were the one. *(Turns to* JAMES*)* You're the one I want to see! What do you mean by making the young ladies of our world-famous summer camp pull you in a wagon all over town? What do you mean? And as for that son of yours—

JAMES. Miss Shaughnessy—control yourself. I don't have a son.

MISS SHAUGHNESSY. And don't lie. I can't stand liars. I think your behavior has been shameful. And if I ever lay hands on the man who was cracking that whip over their poor innocent heads—

TONY. *(Edging toward hall)* Well—I gotta go now.

MISS SHAUGHNESSY. *(In a shout to shake the rafters)* Monkeyface! (TONY *freezes*) Monkeyface— what are you doing here?

TONY. *(Swallowing, steps downstage)* Mr. Clark, I want you to know my girl friend, Miss Shaughnessy. *(As though in apology)* I said she was Irish.

MISS SHAUGHNESSY. Monkeyface—what are you doing in this house?

TONY. *(In a little voice)* Frances—prepare yourself. I—I—I cracked the whip.

MISS SHAUGHNESSY. You what?

TONY. Over their heads, remember. I cracked the whip. But I was very careful.

MISS SHAUGHNESSY. *(Starts slowly for* TONY, *who retreats to Right)* Monkeyface—I'm going to tear you apart—

TONY. *(As he dashes out)* Oh, Fuss-budget— *(Then very swiftly because* MISS SHAUGHNESSY *is getting close)* I just want to say I had a very fine time— *(He dashes out French doors,* MISS SHAUGHNESSY *on his heels.)*

MISS SHAUGHNESSY. You'll have a better time if I ever get hold of that whip! *(She has gone.)*

BILL. *(Appears in the hall. Pleasantly)* The door was open, so I—

*(*HARRIET *and* PAMELA, *in a single movement, whirl and start for hall.)*

PAMELA. Bill!
BILL. Hullo.
HARRIET. Bill Henly!
BILL. *(Equally pleasant)* Hello!

*(*BILL *moves down to Center,* HARRIET *on one side,* PAMELA *on the other. In the kitchen the dog* BARKS *for joy.* BILL *is smiling as he approaches* JAMES, *who is slightly Left of Center.)*

BILL. I've just come from the Club, sir.

*(*MR. MORGAN *lifts his head.)*

JAMES. *(Pointing)* There's Mr. Morgan.
BILL. *(Turning; politely)* How do you do, sir? *(Then to* JAMES*)* The votes have all been counted.
PAMELA. *(Impulsively)* Bill—where have you been?
BILL. I had to have a chance to think.
MR. MORGAN. Well—?
HARRIET. But where did you go?
BILL. I got in my old jalopy and took a little trip all by myself—so I could think.
HELEN. Bill—you said the votes had been counted—
PAMELA. But I've been so worried, Bill.
HARRIET. So have I.
BILL. I'm sorry.
MR. MORGAN. Young man—can't you keep your mind on one thing at a time?

BILL. Not when they're both so pretty, Mr. Morgan.

MR. MORGAN. I don't mean that—I mean the election.

PAMELA. Did you make any decisions, Bill?

BILL. Several. For one thing, I'm going away to college in the fall.

SONNY. Listen, Bud—right now we're not interested in your education. What about the votes?

BILL. Oh, yeah. Well—

HARRIET. I can tell by your eyes, Mr. Henly. I know. *(Crosses to* MR. MORGAN*)* And I blame you entirely! *(She turns and crosses to hall.)*

BILL. *(Following her)* I'm awfully sorry, Harriet. You see, I decided to go to Columbia—

PAMELA. Columbia—why, that's right in New York City! *(She runs up to hall.)*

BILL. I know.

HARRIET. *(To* PAMELA*)* I don't blame him, Pamela.

PAMELA. Oh, I'm sorry, Harriet.

HARRIET. It's all right. *(Near tears)* I've been a heel. I know it— Just like my father. *(She goes out.)*

(BILL *and* PAMELA *stand facing each other.)*

BETSY. I'm going cuckoo! Why doesn't he *say* something?

MR. MORGAN. *(Rising and starting after* HARRIET*)* Did you hear what she said? Is that what I seem to her? My own daughter?

HELEN. Bill Henly! If you don't tell us—

BILL. *(Taking his eyes from* PAMELA, *but holding her hand; turns to room)* Oh, yeah—the election. Well, you won all right, Mr.—

MR. MORGAN. That doesn't matter now. *(Crosses to hall, past* BILL *and* PAMELA*)* I cede the election to you, Clark.

BILL. You don't need to, Mr. Morgan. He won anyway.

(There are general exclamations of delight, ad lib.

BETSY *and* ESTHER *turn to* SONNY *and hug him.*
SONNY *sinks to the up Right chair, too weak for
words.* HELEN *crosses to* JAMES *and goes into his
arms. Then* MR. MORGAN *returns to* JAMES; *offers
his hand. He is sincere and disturbed.)*

(WARN Curtain.)

MR. MORGAN. Mr. Clark—I congratulate you. Maybe
the people have a sense of humor after all— I'm going
to develope one myself. *(Turns to* PAMELA*)* And if my
paper ever gets out of line—you let me know. *(To*
JAMES*)* And you can count on me in the fall—

(So far JAMES *hasn't opened his mouth. He has let
MR. MORGAN shake his hand; he has received a
hug from* HELEN*. But he stands dumbly, staring
ahead.* MR. MORGAN *goes out front door. All eyes
are on* JAMES*. Slowly he wilts, as though in a
faint.* HELEN *catches him and* BILL *crosses to
assist. They help him, as he staggeringly tries to
walk, to the sofa, all this amid ad lib. exclamations: "Open his collar— It's the strain— He
hasn't been eating right— Lift up his feet— Careful, now—" And so forth.* SONNY, ESTHER *and
BETSY bend over back of sofa.* BILL *and* PAMELA
have moved to Right of sofa.)

JAMES. *(On sofa)* Did you hear what he said?
HELEN. You won, darling. You *won!*
JAMES. What did you call me?
HELEN. *Darling*—you won!
LESLIE. That sounds like goodbye to me. *(He crosses
to hall.)*
HELEN. *(Calling after* LESLIE*)* Goodbye, Leslie!

*(LESLIE goes out front door. But as he goes, he almost
bumps headlong into LILLIAN and CLIFFORD, who
enter quickly.)*

LILLIAN. My children! My dear, dear children! We

missed you so much we had to— *(Sees them bending over* JAMES *on sofa)* What's happened? What is it?

(She and CLIFFORD *are at Center.)*

CLIFFORD. I'm not a bit surprised! He's collapsed. I meant to do it years ago.

JAMES. I feel fine. *(But his voice sounds weak. He blinks at* HELEN*)* Darling— *(He closes his eyes again.)*

SONNY. *(To* BETSY *and* ESTHER*)* Listen, kids— we'll all three go to the Ball. We'll wow 'em!

LILLIAN. Don't worry, Jimmie—we're going to take them right away.

JAMES. *(Sitting up, his feet still on sofa)* Let them stay, Lillian. Let them stay forever!

CLIFFORD. He's delirious.

PAMELA. *(A new thought has struck her)* Sonny— the fall elections!

SONNY. Don't worry. I'll take care of everything. *(He crosses to Center, all eyes on him)* Now listen, everyone—we'll all have to cooperate if Unc's going to be District Attorney! The first thing to do—we'll stage the biggest rally this town has even seen! The biggest show this *State* has ever seen! ! !

JAMES. *(Closes his eyes and sinks back on sofa— weakly)* No— No— No— Make him shut up, somebody.

SONNY. I got it all worked out in my head—

(But before he can go on,

THE CURTAIN HAS FALLEN SWIFTLY

QUIET SUMMER

PROPERTY PLOT

ACT ONE

On desk:
    Telephone.
    Desk set.
    Paper, etc.
    Portable typewriter.
Trophies on mantel.
Telegram (HELEN).
Desk calendar (JAMES).
Notebook, pencil (HELEN).
Books.
Bowl of string beans (CARRIE).
Box
Delivery-pad   } (TONY).
Reducing machine
Luggage
Golf clubs } (SONNY).
Radio
Luggage
Tennis racquets
Hat boxes } (PAMELA).
Typewriter
Hairpin (HELEN).

ACT TWO

Posters.
Tennis racquets.
Golf clubs.
Fencing foils.

Sweaters.
Sneakers.
Records.
Sandwiches.
Fruit.
Two packages ⎱ (TONY).
Delivery book ⎰
Flash camera (FREDERICKA).
Machine parts ⎱ (SONNY).
Screw-driver ⎰
Box of costumes (TONY).
Whip (in box).
Crepe paper (JEANIE, BETSY, ESTHER).
Traveling-bag (CARRIE).

ACT THREE

Whip (TONY).
Camera (FREDERICKA).

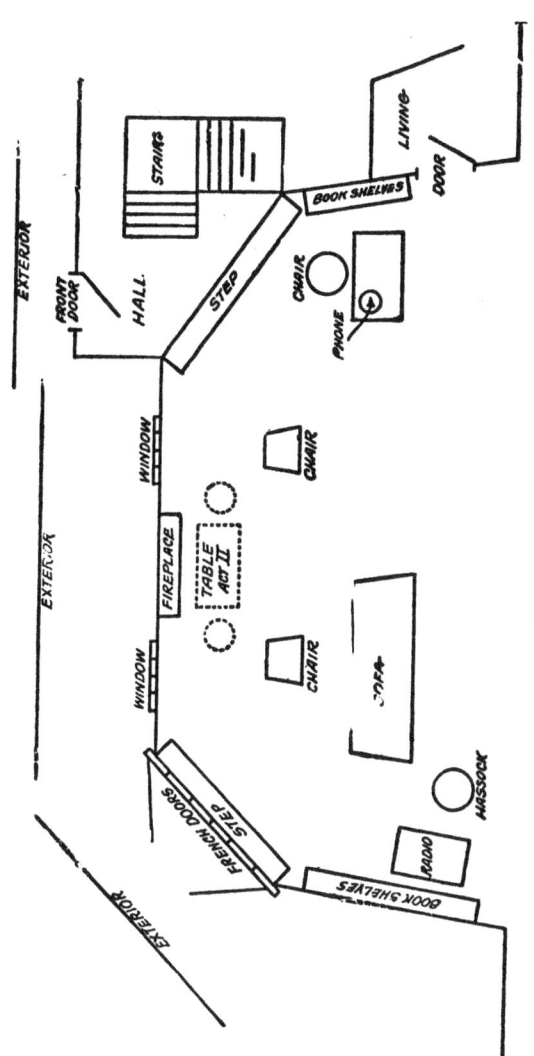

SCENE DESIGN

"QUIET SUMMER"